DARKENED
MINDS

DARKENED MINDS

GARY LEE VINCENT

Burning Bulb
PUBLISHING

Darkened Minds
By **Gary Lee Vincent**

Burning Bulb Publishing
P.O. Box 4721
Bridgeport, WV 26330-4721
www.BurningBulbPublishing.com

Edition ISBN

        Paperback 978-0-69266-981-5

First edition.
Printed in the United States of America.

Library of Congress Control Number: 2016904392

PART 1

JACKIE

PROLOGUE

THE RED BEAST OF HELL
6,660 B.C.

And I beheld when he had opened the sixth seal, and, lo, there was a great earthquake; and the sun became black as sackcloth of hair, and the moon became as blood;

And the stars of heaven fell unto the earth, even as a fig tree casteth her untimely figs, when she is shaken of a mighty wind.

And the heaven departed as a scroll when it is rolled together; and every mountain and island were moved out of their places.

And the kings of the earth, and the great men, and the rich men, and the chief captains, and the mighty men, and every bondman, and every free man, hid themselves in the dens and in the rocks of the mountains;

And said to the mountains and rocks, "Fall on us, and hide us from the face of him that sitteth on the throne, and from the wrath of the Lamb: For the great day of his wrath is come; and who shall be able to stand?"

Revelation 6, verses 12-17

Massive hailstones shot down and hit the earth as the fiery thunderstorm persisted. The inhabitants had taken cover long ago. Most of them. Those who were left. Despite the hail being made of blood – but frozen solid, with each stone the size of a dollar coin – each hailstone burned with an incendiary force, streaking through the air like flaming fireworks, setting fire to trees wherever it hit them and burning up all the lush green grass, leaving frazzled black wires like sparse pubic hair in the scorched and blood-soaked earth. From the first strikes, the fire burned with an unnatural power and consumed all in its path, eating up all living things and covering the earth with thick pools of coagulated blood that slowly dried to dark, scorched bloodstains.

"They don't stand a chance against this," Victor said to himself, his brow furrowed in deep concern. His mind reeled, trying to comprehend what these small communities of humans could do, faced with such destructive power. How do you battle the elements? How do you fight pure evil?

A massive roaring sound diverted Victor's attention, and the earth vibrated as a great loud rumbling persisted. A huge mountain, all aflame and burning dry with a vicious fierceness, split down one side, cracked into rocky shards and its sheer cliffs slid and crumbled into the sea. Parts of all the oceans of the world unaccountably became blood, choking up all the living creatures in the sea, leaving them gasping desperately to breathe or move until they died a horrific suffocating death. A third of all the sailing ships were tossed around on thirty-foot waves and destroyed in great storms – all

4

hands lost, in the tumultuous, scarlet waves of the relentlessly rolling waters.

Victor's hand was pressed to his mouth, aghast. His wings, dyed raven-black and besmirched with soot from the battles and expulsion he had suffered during the Great Rebellion, were folded hard against his shoulders, held tight and flat as if for protection. Strong as he was, Victor hoped to make himself as small as possible; to go unnoticed. Because he was as powerless as anyone against the horror that was unfolding before him.

The Red Beast of Hell was on the rampage. Only God could help them now. And God had turned his back on humankind, for all their sin and selfishness. Ironically, the Red Beast of Hell, under Lucifer's command, was doing God's work for him. *What will be, will be. If civilization is destroyed – if the face of the earth is wiped clean – that is all the better, for making a fresh start.*

A huge great star, burning like fire, fell down from the skies. Watching it hurtle towards the earth, closer and even larger, people screamed and ran for shelter. But the worst of it was not the shattering impact that knocked the earth off its axis, vibrating like an after-shock across the continents. The effects were more pervasive than that. The small planet or asteroid that hit earth was itself composed of a dangerous poison that infected a third of all the rivers, the springs, pools, lakes and waterways of the world, and tarnished them with its toxic waste. The reservoir areas from which a vast proportion of the population sourced their drinking water became filled with the bitter poison, and all of these people died from drinking these dangerous toxins,

5

having no other water available to sustain them. Their choice was to die of thirst or die of poison – a long, lingering and desperate death whichever choice they made. A third of the global population was killed by these inescapable factors, and a great wailing and weeping went on in the world as the suffering spread.

Blackness had hit the earth. A third of the sun, moon, and all the stars were darkened – even at the height of the day, and neither the day nor the night were illuminated for a third of their duration. Plunged into black shadow and oppressive gloom for all or much of the time, the crops could not grow, and another third of the people died agonising deaths of belly-aching hunger. But all of this had just been the beginning.

Filled with horror, Victor gazed out over the devastation below him, his mouth fallen open. He could not help but exclaim involuntarily, "Woe, woe, woe, to the inhabitants of the earth!"

The Red Beast of Hell had been unleashed on the world, and its devastation was present in every respect – whether in air, sea, land, or in the hearts of men. And how was anyone to defend themselves from something so elemental as weather or intangible as suicidal thoughts and despairing emotions? There was no escape. No hope.

There were many who had believed that the wrath of God had been too harsh – the rules too stringent – the situation impossible for angel or man to bear. To Victor, the sins for which people had been punished by God were all very mild indeed – greed, fornication, avarice and blasphemy. Indeed, many of the angels practised these things themselves. Resentment grew. It had caused a great rift in the heavens and the angels themselves were divided in their loyalties. Led by the Archangel Lucifer, who felt himself equal – if not superior – to God, a great rebellion had taken place. On the side of God, Archangel Michael and his multitude of angels had fought valiantly against Lucifer and his hordes of dark angel followers. There had been a bloody war in heaven, and the great beast or dragon-serpent, along with Lucifer (also called the Devil or Satan), and his own dark angels, of which Victor was one, had been violently flung out of heaven. Now that the dark angels had been cast out, the impact of that battle and Lucifer's evil had spread to earth. While the heavenly angels regrouped and recuperated, and while God allowed Lucifer to enable people to show people their true colors and declare their loyalties – to their ultimate destruction, evil spread over the earth.

Lucifer's shapeshifting evil took many guises, from snake to reptilian dragon and more, in his attempts to constantly deceive the whole world, to beguile and overthrow God and others. With Lucifer's pure evil essence now in the form of the Red Beast of Hell – literally, all hell was let loose on the planet.

Victor had watched another angel fall to the earth, just as he himself had done. It was Abaddon, an arrogant self-seeking creature, who held in his skeletal fingers the key to the bottomless pit, given to him by Lucifer, to fulfil his duty to him. But this task and ownership of this key, Abaddon presumed, gave him great power – power enough to rival Lucifer, he had thought.

Victor watched his old compatriot immediately unlock the door to the bottomless pit, to reveal the fiery gates of hell, before pronouncing himself king. "I hereby rule the bottomless pit!" Abaddon announced, grinning widely with a thin-lipped leer. "I command this realm, as King of Darkness!"

But Abaddon would soon pay for his hubris. There was no king who could take command over this chaos. Not when the Red Beast of Hell had been unleashed. Because the fallen angel, Lucifer, was as wrathful as God. And worse. Abaddon was immediately swept up in the air, screaming; his limbs tumbling and his red robes flying. He was flung bodily into the burning torments of hell, where he was slowly torn limb from limb, only to be reconstructed, then to be ripped apart again, over and over, for all eternity. And his ear-piercing screeches of pain echoed in the air.

Known by many names and taking many different forms, the shapeshifter Lucifer was the embodiment of true evil. This being was the diametric opposite of love and caring: the darkness in contrast to the light. The angel Lucifer – who had started out as the very definition of goodness, his name meaning 'bearer of light' – having been cast down to earth, was now known by many titles – Satan, the Devil, Beelzebub, Baal, Lord of Darkness – and he took many shapes – from the horned god, to far more. He could be an indescribably terrifying beast; a normal, mild-mannered human being – or an invisible evil. He was a singular creature, and yet he could divide himself up into a multitude of insects, animals or humans – or would simply create an intangible atmosphere of discomfort, pain, anger, depression or wickedness. He was nowhere to be seen, and yet he could be everywhere; taking hold within everyone who would allow a touch of evil in their hearts. No one was safe, then. No one is safe, now.

When The Fall came, Lucifer was flung to the earth, and his angels were cast out with him, their wings marked black to signify their disloyalty. His long, lashing tail had whipped down with it a third of the stars from heaven, casting them down to the earth. This was a third of the angels – of whom Victor was just one small, insignificant minor player. Victor had made a conscious decision, according to his own moral compass – and he had chosen the path of evil. His lord and master was Lucifer, to be sure, but for himself, Victor was beneath Lucifer's contempt. He was just one of the many dark followers, but he was happy to keep a low profile and to go unnoticed – unlike Abaddon. Victor certainly did not want to suffer a similar fate. Indeed, no one had seen the true power of Lucifer up to this point, and Victor was terrified enough by all he had witnessed so far. Indeed, he was afraid of following him too closely.

The bottomless pit was now opened and an all-encompassing cloud of dense black smoke billowed out from the great furnace of hell below. The smoke from the pit was so thick and impenetrable that the sun and the air were darkened by it, compounding the blackness with the general shadow that had fallen on the earth even at midday. Already, the screams of tortured souls emanated from the gaping hole, and more humans were being flung down there in their thousands.

Out of the black smoke, in a whirring cloud of stiff, wooden wings rattling like a thousand chariots in battle, came a swarm of powerful locusts, each the size of a warhorse and armored in iron breastplates. The air was thick with their bulky bodies and great flapping wings. These locusts were an ugly parody of humankind as if genetically crossed with insects and animals: with long streaming hair, human faces and vicious jaws with sharp teeth like lions' that could have ripped out the throats of strong men if they chose to. They each had a stinging scorpion tail which arched above their heads, tipped with poison, with the ability to leave someone in a paroxysm of pain for a whole five months after an attack. In a great, clattering rattle, they swooped down upon any visible human – and often broke down doors – to bite or sting them – and although they could have picked off the flesh of a body within five minutes, they did not kill. Carnivorous as they were, they ignored the sparse vegetation that was left on the earth, and set out instead to torture humankind, simply biting into their flesh and sucking out sufficient blood to leave them in pain, but alive. The humans' feeble weapons of sticks, stones and knives were as useless as kisses against these creatures' heavily armored skin and superhuman strength, so the victims flailed helplessly, uselessly, against them. The hell-born locusts did not kill them outright, but for a whole five months gave them a torment of pain like the constant stinging of a thousand bees. That was far worse than death and almost unbearable. Men sought to kill themselves and cried out to be put out of their misery, but they could find no blessed release. Death evaded them. They were the living dead.

Victor watched with interest, fascinated and appalled. Despite the horror, it struck him that these ugly human-locust creatures were so much more than violent killers: they tasted human blood for the thrill and enjoyment of it. They could bestow a kiss of long-lasting pain that affected people very deeply, shaking them to the core of their being. Despite the chaos below, from a position of safety that derived from his distant standpoint and gave him some objectivity, Victor coldly witnessed the world in disarray, making mental notes for the future. His future. There was something profoundly attractive in these winged creatures' almost sexual predation. The fact that they pursued humans by flying through the air, sweeping down their great bat-like wings and landing on top of their prey, dashing them to the earth and using their sharp teeth and tails to tease them to the edge of death… but not quite. Victor sensed their power and control – even from such a distance. Despite the degree of detachment that enabled him to analyse the whole situation, he still felt a direct, visceral thrill of power and sexual stimulation surging through his own body. His eyes widened, and his body trembled with excitement. It was as if he could taste the blood himself, warm, metallic and nourishing – giving him a sense of self – a sense of eternal life. And that seminal feeling would affect Victor's destiny forever, hereafter, for all the centuries that he would live.

Then, four angels on horseback were released, in command of an army of 200,000,000 warriors with the fierce intention of slaying a third of humankind. But these were no heavenly angels, as Victor had been. They wore breastplates of raging fire, jacinth, and brimstone. Every individual hair of their horses' tails was a sinuous snake with sharp, venomous fangs that could kill with one bite, should anyone get close enough. These bundles of snakes writhed in the air and entwined around one another, their metallic scaly bodies glistening in dark iridescent rainbows like oil in water, their mouths wide with fangs exposed expectantly, and their pebble-black eyes soulless. But no one would get close enough to give the snakes their due and satisfy their craving for blood. The horses had lions' heads and they breathed out fifteen-foot bursts of hot fire, smoke and sulphurous-smelling brimstone, which choked and killed all in their path.

If the plagues of fire, floods, weather, blood, locusts, death and war did not kill people, there was worse to come.

The Red Beast of Hell had arrived. These locust creatures of torment and warriors were merely the warm-up acts to the main event – presaging the utter horror of the Beast's presence. It had taken its most monstrous form: the shape of a fearsome seven-headed red dragon – each thrashing head the size of a mountain, each cruelly-taloned foot large enough to crush an entire country beneath its scaly tread. Each one of its seven heads was uglier than the one before it, but the worst and largest of all had a vicious serrated beak and sharp, multiple rows of razor-like teeth, each tooth a metal forest in itself. Every one of its fourteen flashing red eyes burned with a raging fire reminiscent of the pit of hell itself. It breathed out fire and brimstone: the most pungent smell of rotten eggs and decaying flesh. When it opened its vast, leathery wings, it encompassed a whole continent. Its massive presence blocked out all the light, grotesque and threatening, roaring mightily from its seven scaly throats so that the very earth trembled, let alone its inhabitants. Its heavy heads swept around on the long stems of their muscular, snake-like necks, scouring the landscape, searching out prey. Anyone would do. Anything.

Victor stood horrified, frozen to the spot but involuntarily shaking in fear. There was no escape from this horror. So petrified was he that he did not even feel the warm rush of urine as he wet himself.

Atop their thick, sinuous necks, the great red dragon's seven vicious heads were each crowned with ugly iron headwear, their royal status representing dominion over an entire continent. Ten jagged, dangerous horns, along with the snarling, gnashing sharp teeth filled everyone with fear. For those remaining humans or disobedient dark angels – Victor included, if he was not careful – there was no escape from the Red Beast of Hell.

Even in the face of death, life vainly attempted to go on. But wherever a mother was giving birth, one head of the dragon peered down on them. The dragon's mouth slavered before each pregnant woman in labor who was ready to be delivered, preparing itself to devour their children as soon as they were born. Helplessly, the women cried and screamed in pain and terror, unable to stop nature's course, and unable to save themselves or their child; but sweating and moaning, in a flood of blood and afterbirth, their legacy and life slithered out of them, into the gaping maws of the Red Beast. New-born babies were considered a delicacy, because Lucifer loathed sinlessness and loved nothing more than to destroy innocence. Even the two-seconds-old, pure, new baby was not spared, but became a miniscule, barely-discernible snack of fresh-blooded flesh, soft yielding skin and pliable greenstick bones that made barely a snap, so young were they. The Red Beast's forked tongue always slid up the still-attached umbilical cord, and dragged the bloodied, grief-stricken mother into its mouth after it, incapacitated as she was.

Even Victor was sickened to the stomach, and held his hand over his mouth, hoping to contain the acidic-tasting bile rising within his throat. This was nothing – this was just the tiniest detail in a global terror of epic proportions. It seemed that the very world itself would be destroyed, and Victor was paralyzed. He remained distraught and completely immobile, afraid to move for fear of drawing attention to himself. He wanted to stay alive for as long as he could. Both God and Lucifer had promised him immortality. But what he had seen would change him forever. He had witnessed the terrible vengeance of God, and also of the Devil. He hardly knew which was worse. He feared both.

This slaughtering of innocents was all too much for anyone to bear. A huge, earth-shattering roar of anger rent the skies in two, which Victor recognized as the voice of God. It shocked everyone, and stopped even the Red Beast of Hell in his tracks.

Suddenly, in the darkest moment, when all had given up hope and all seemed lost, an ethereal but blinding light shot through the darkness. Shocked and blinded by the spontaneous searing whiteness, Victor squinted his eyes closed. He had no choice – it was just too extreme a brightness. Simultaneously, from the tear in the dark clouds, the ear-splitting harmonious voices of a multitudinous choir of angels broke out, ripping through the thickened atmosphere.

Accompanied by these heavenly voices singing the harmony of the spheres, and out of the heavens, there shone a gigantic woman: all white, silver and gold – and enrobed in the very sunlight itself, with the moon shining huge beneath her feet, and wearing a crown of twelve stars upon her head. His eyelids throbbing, Victor tentatively opened his eyes, and found it difficult to focus until his vision adjusted itself to accommodate the shimmering glare of her presence. It was almost unbearable to look at her, the brightness was so painful; but with her, she also brought an overwhelming sensation of love and a momentary quiet, stillness, and peace. It did not last.

Recovered from his surprise and roaring a loud battle-cry, the Red Beast of Hell rose up out of the sea, with great cascades of bloody water frothing with pink foam falling from his wings and heads, back into the cloying and coagulated blood sea. The heavenly woman pointed towards the Beast's largest head with one straight finger, and a massive thunderbolt of light burst forth from the tip of her fingernail, with a thunderous crack of explosive electricity. The lightning struck the Beast with a massive crash and blinding light; but although one of his heads was wounded so fatally that it was a mere shattered mass of blood and shreds of skin, raw shards of bone visible on the stem of its ugly neck, its other six heads and ten horns otherwise hardly wavered. In fact, before Victor's very eyes, the Beast's deadly wound grew remarkably healed within seconds, and the entire head grew back as if new. In a flash, the beast changed into a huge leopard with the feet of a bear, and the mouths of seven lions, and it stood strong again, with great power and authority and gave seven mighty roars of fire, which projected forcefully towards the vision of the lady in a massive fireball. The woman receded and melted away into the heavens, leaving only a hopeful light in her wake.

Struck by awe, the vast majority of the dark angels and even most of the remaining humans, fearing Lucifer's wrath, fell down and worshipped the dragon beast, saying, "Who else is like the Beast?"

They bowed their heads and muttered amongst themselves, "Who could possibly win a war against him?" and "He is unbeatable. All-powerful."

Even the ones whose hearts were good at the base of it all were fearful and thought to themselves, "We had better obey, and do whatever he bids us."

"Quake, earth-dwellers!" the mighty beast roared, its seven cruel beaks wide open, revealing vicious teeth dripping blood. "Bow down to me, as the representative of your lord and master, Lucifer!"

All the individuals of humankind who valued their lives, and the dark angels who valued their existence, bowed their heads lower still, in worship and deference to the Beast, and out of sheer terror.

And, encouraged by this obedience and filled with great egotistical power, the Red Beast of Hell opened his dragon-mouth and spoke Lucifer's words in blasphemy against God, cursing him and those who worshipped him, and the remaining angels in heaven. "All that dwell upon the earth shall worship ME!" he roared, as an ending to his diatribe, his seven mouths exclaiming his hatred of God and virtue, in a booming chorus of voices.

To emphasise this, a great fireball came crashing down onto the earth from heaven and there was a great wailing of fear and distress from the crowds who saw these miracles. Lucifer had deceived them all, and God was furious – so they hardly knew which way to turn.

"Worship my image, and live!" the voices of the Red Beast boomed. "Anyone who does not worship me will be killed." The audience prostrated themselves on the ground, not wishing to defy the beast on Lucifer's command, pouring his verbal poison into the ears of his listeners. "If you are wise, you will count the number of the Beast, which is also the number of a man, and that number is six hundred and sixty-six."

But the heavens suddenly ripped apart, opened up again like a silken cloth in a great, wide-open tear, accompanied by those booming heavenly voices whose high vibrations shook the very souls of men. In a blaze of light, a massively large white horse came galloping out of heaven, with a powerful man riding on its back, whose name was The Word of God, Faithful and True. He was dressed all in white, but his robes had been dipped in fresh blood that dripped from its hems, leaving a dancing ribbon of scarlet blood in the air in his wake, and his long brown hair streamed out behind him in the rushing wind of his traveling. On his head he wore many crowns, with a name written on them in a curious language that no one understood, so that no man knew his name, except for himself.

"I am come to judge all sinners and to make war on Satan!" he cried, his eyes aflame with a raging fire, raising his blazing sword aloft.

The people screamed in terror. Having fallen down at the Red Beast's feet to protect themselves, they now realized that they might have made a mistake in pinning their colors to the Devil's mast. In the split seconds that followed, individuals re-made their choices and chose their sides – each hoping to back the winner. Some who had recently fallen down before the Devil's own now rallied again, and were determined to join forces with the powers of good.

And the armies from heaven followed the shining lead horseman, all of them mounted on white horses, too, and all clothed in white, clean, fine linen – that was pure and symbolic of their goodness. Their numbers were countless, and from the distance they made a great, streaming white flying carpet of snow, like an avalanche from the skies, pouring down on the dark, ruined earth, white banners flying. The dark forces were appalled by this magnificent yet terrifying sight.

Brandishing a sharp sword, with fierceness and wrath, the nameless horse-rider came thundering down to confront the armies of darkness led by the Red Beast of Hell, and all who worshipped him. As the glorious horseman approached, despite the speed of his galloping horse and the distance from which Victor observed events, Victor could still clearly read the words written on the man's billowing robes: "KING OF KINGS, AND LORD OF LORDS", and Victor quaked in fear, because he knew what this meant. Even the Red Beast of Hell responded in alarm, his seven heads rearing back in the air and recoiling towards his shrunken, cowering body.

As the multitude of white horsemen assembled in the skies, one glorious angel stood within the glaring light of the sun itself, and cried out with a loud voice, saying to all on earth, "Come and gather yourselves together for the supper of the great God! None shall escape, and all will be killed and consumed as meat by the righteous, in punishment for their evil alliance with the Devil. You may eat the flesh of kings, and the flesh of captains, and the flesh of mighty men, and the flesh of horses, and the flesh of those who sit on them, and the flesh of all men, both free and bound in slavery, both insignificant and greatly famous. None who side with the devil shall escape!"

The Red Beast of Hell gave a loud cry of anger from his seven mouths, heads thrown back and vicious-teethed jaws wide open, ready to attack. The plague of horse-sized locusts took to the air and burst into action, as did the dark angels, the skies a-whirr with their black wings. But not Victor, who remained between the two worlds, frozen in horror; a helpless observer.

The great thundering sound of a thousand billion mighty hooves filled the air, as the hordes of strong white horses with their powerful angelic riders galloped down, bearing their unsheathed swords of light and justice, steadily pointing their deadly blades at the evil to be destroyed.

And the Beast himself, and the kings of the earth who had chosen Lucifer's side, and their armies and supporters all quickly gathered together, prepared to go into battle for the forces of evil in this war against the white horseman representing God himself, and against his armies of angels and his virtuous human followers.

Except for Victor, who stood alone, out of sight. For protection of himself, for fear, and out of a morbid scientific curiosity, he stood observing. *Who else, except God, would have such an overview?* But he quickly dismissed these thoughts – because whichever side was taken in this war, God or Devil would punish such godlike thoughts of overweening pride.

As the stampeding white horses met the black armies, there was an uproarious noise: a great clashing of arms and a cacophony of shouts, screams, groans and war-noise. Death, pain and suffering were everywhere as weapons hacked angels, demons and humans into pieces. This one battle persisted for many days, with the Red Beast and evil forces under relentless fire from the arrows of virtue constantly fired by ten thousand angelic archers, forever re-filling their quivers with more, and firing them fearlessly at their prey. Meanwhile, powerful electrical lightning persistently struck the seven heads of the Beast. Because Lucifer controlled all evil with his mind, this constant attack on his prime vehicle of his will was causing Lucifer great pain, making it difficult to focus his evil and control his wicked troops. He weakened, and his enemies took their advantage. The air was thick with the spray of blood, and wet with the sweat and tears of battle. The white robes of the angelic armies quickly turned scarlet, drenched with the blood of their enemies, and the ground was heavy with piles of bodies, so that those left alive were forced to tread on corpses to fight, their ankles turning as they struggled to maintain their balance, tripping and wading through flesh and bone some four feet deep.

As the forces of God and all that was good gradually found more favor, under this relentless onslaught, the exhausted Beast was worn down, driven low and eventually taken hostage. As was Lucifer himself, gnashing his teeth, in defeat. Naturally, despite his own capture and bone-tiredness, Lucifer was still slippery, and had the capacity to take many forms – but the holy armies of good were wise to his wiles and they ensured that they captured him wholly, entwining him in blessed heavenly silver and gold chains, heavy with purity, which made him powerless and silent. He was the false prophet who performed deceptive miracles, and all those who worshipped his image would suffer a similar fate.

The Beast was captured and flung alive into a lake of fire, burning with sulphurous brimstone that made old wounds raw again and opened up new ones. Unable to make any sound with his forked and deceiving tongue, the Red Beast felt utter extreme and everlasting pain, but was unable to express it.

Victor then saw an angel come down from heaven, holding the key of the bottomless pit. The angel took the battered Lucifer down, and there, he shut him up, locked him in and set a seal upon him, announcing, "This Lucifer, the Devil or Satan, shall deceive the nations no more, till one thousand years should be fulfilled."

"What happens then?" asked Archangel Michael.

"And after that," the Angel with the key to the pit of hell said grimly, "The Devil must be let loose."

21

Lucifer's remaining evil followers were slain with swords of goodness, and at last, those who wished to, could now feast on their flesh, as promised.

Exhausted by consistent watching, Victor stood trembling, unable to move, since he did not know which way to turn. He could not bring himself to declare himself a follower of God and his goodness again. Heaven, love and virtue sickened him. But neither could he fully ally himself with the mindless violence of Lucifer and the Red Beast of Hell. Nor would he allow himself to be cast down into the pits of hell, with the other dark angels and demons. Visiting hell was as far as he would go – he didn't want to remain there. Victor was in a quandary. He wanted to stay on the earth, live a long life, be his own master and exact his own form of evil. Do the Devil's work in his own quiet way, from the earth plane. Those blood-sucking flying creatures had affected him profoundly, given him ideas. His black wings twitched in anticipation. But whatever happened, if he lived long enough, he needed to do all he could to prevent the Red Beast of Hell from being unleashed again with such extreme destructive force. It had been so devastating, it should never occur again. He shuddered at the thought.

And then the angel laid hands on the Beast of Hell, the dragon, pulling him up out of the lake of fire, only to bind him up with heavy iron holy chains for nine thousand years, and cast him deep into the bottomless pit. There he shut him up, locked him in and set an immovable seal upon him, announcing, "This Red Beast of Hell shall carry out Lucifer's work no more, till nine thousand years should be fulfilled."

They weren't to know that someone would inadvertently attempt to release this hellish Beast only eight thousand, six hundred and eighty years later.

CHAPTER 1

PRESENT DAY

The Darkness all around them was soft and thick with an almost tangible density to it. There was no breeze nor way of orientating oneself – just a cloying dampness in the air, like a moldy blanket enshrouding all of them as they tried to move forward. Kate opened her mouth to it, and discerned on her tongue a definite texture to the atmosphere. She bared her newly emerged fangs in the dark, testing them. She felt she could almost take a bite out of the air – an odd feeling, but no more odd than the series of events that had led her here.

Stumbling in the pitch darkness like a lamb to the slaughter, the captive Victor Rothenstein seethed. As if it were not bad enough that he had been forced to give Jackie Nixon and her daughter, Kate, the vampiric immortality they had demanded at silver gunpoint; but now, the two women were leading him by the neck on a leash in the most undignified manner. Against his will and better judgement, Victor was having to obey their every word, as he and the two women proceeded deeper into the Darkness.

Unknown to all of them – although Victor had an inkling, and certainly a hope of it – William followed on behind them, unseen, and at a discreet distance. The darkness was so thick and cloying, muffling sound as well as sight, that it was only by straining his ears and following their voices that William had a good idea of where the others had gone before him, enabling him to pursue them.

Clinging firmly to that hope, whenever silence fell between the three vampires, alert to the danger of William losing them, Victor would raise his voice with some inconsequential words or phrases.

"You'll never get away with this," he cried, from time to time.

"Oh, I think you'll find that we will," Jackie said bitterly.

As time went on, she became increasingly irritated by his inane mutterings and outcries. Victor seemed to be filling any silence with words just for the sake of conversation, and she needed to concentrate.

"Where do you want me to go now?" Victor asked.

Jackie came to a sudden stop, jerking the studded collar around Victor's neck with the abruptness of the taut leash preventing him from stepping any further forward. His tongue involuntarily protruded and he made a gargling noise as he choked from the constriction around his throat.

"What the hell are you talking about?" Jackie snarled. "You know damn fine where we're going."

Victor shrugged. "Nerves," he offered.

Jackie Nixon's red eyes blazed at him, even in the darkness. She did not for one moment believe him, but she had no idea, otherwise, what his game was.

***

For his part, William concentrated on the sound of the primary voices he was following, and the black-on-black outlines of their figures he could just make out as his eyes adjusted. But all around him, there were other noises in the background: the sounds of distant moanings and sighing, and the wispy gray insubstantial figures that passed in the distance. If William lost focus for one second, he feared he would lose Kate and the others forever.

He still couldn't help thinking of Kate as 'my Kate', despite the fact that she had betrayed him, and worse still, was now a fully-fledged vampire. He no longer trusted her, but there was still a residual emotion there, for the tender and loving young woman she had been. She looked the same: pretty girl, with fair hair… But he shook his head, trying to eliminate those old thoughts. He had work to do, and this meant keeping them in his sights.

And it wasn't just losing them – or Kate – in the dark that was William's problem, because from what Victor had told him, if he didn't follow them, and follow this whole thing through, the world – and possibly the universe – was in danger. And thus, with grim determination, despite his bruises and cuts, William followed them deeper and deeper into the Darkness, knowing that he would have to take action at some point to prevent the evil and earth-shattering ritual that Victor had warned him about.

***

After they had walked a while, that realm's cold pitch-black thinned into a purple light that gently made everything appear fluorescent, their bodies all glowing with an eerie ultraviolet light. An intense glow lay somewhere over the horizon, like a sunrise. Immediately aware of this new phenomenon, William held back further from the group he was following – afraid of being seen now that the nature of the darkness and visibility within it had changed. He still kept his eyes trained on his vampire quarry, but he was conscious to take cover along the way. Fortunately, through the sinister light, a definite, although desolate, landscape within the unknown terrain made itself apparent – including mounds and rocks behind which William could conceal himself as he crept up behind Jackie, Kate and Victor.

As they turned a corner, the landscape levelled out. The odd ultraviolet light emanated from their target on the horizon and the travelers stopped, the strangely luminous glow washing over their faces like a purple dawn. William crouched down behind a boulder, gazing in wonder, too.

Kate gasped aloud.

Only a few hundred yards ahead of them, its tall, spindly turrets scratching the odd, black sky, and bathed in a definite fluorescent purple light, stood an ancient castle. Its structure was imposing, but it had a dilapidated air to it. The massive iron gates were rusted and hanging off their hinges, gaping open like a massive mouth. Thin arrow slits were the only windows visible, giving the face of the building the air of a suspicious frown. The whole castle stood somewhat uncertainly upon a cliff that presided over a dark, stony beach and a barren, gray sea that lazily lapped the shore.

"You know where we are now, I guess?" Jackie asked Victor sarcastically, unable to hide a thrill of excitement in her voice as she gazed at the edifice before her.

"Um-hum," Victor sounded, behind his closed lips.

Jackie yanked Victor's chain again, causing his eyes to bulge and his mouth to open in a sudden cough. She snapped at him, "And what is below?"

His hooded eyes speaking volumes of venom towards her, Victor muttered, "The Vampire City."

"Good boy," sneered Jackie. Then she turned her glowing, eager eyes back to the scene before her, and said, in awe: "Just as legend has it. The Vampire Castle overlooks the immensely old vampire city." She pointed to the landscape of indistinguishable rubble as far as the eye could see. "It was abandoned long ago, and now stands empty, owing to the vampires having fallen asleep under an ancient curse..." Her voice dropped reverently. "But they are not gone – only sleeping." A sinister smile played on her lips.

"Where are they?" asked Kate. "The vampires?"

"They are all in caskets, in subterranean crypts," smiled Jackie, indulgently. "Isn't that right, Victor?"

He said nothing, his lips held tightly together, and therefore, in order to urge him to respond, Jackie snapped the leash in her hand, the leather strap of the dog-collar biting into Victor's Adam's apple.

He tried to turn the jerk of his head into a nod, grunting, "Yes."

"Just waiting for us," Jackie said, her eyes shining like a child in a candy shop. She led Victor by the chain, and beckoned Kate forward, to approach the castle.

William watched from the distance, biting his lip in concern. His best bet was to follow them and find Victor – if he was ever left alone – and discover what he should do next. For all William's ecclesiastical training, research and his practical experience in battling vampires, zombies and other evil, he really had no idea what he was up against this time, or how best to approach it. However, he had an idea that a small phial of holy water wasn't going to cut it, in this case. Much as Victor Rothenstein was his enemy, William needed all the help and expert insight he could get.

Having entered the hefty but inadequate gates, the small group of vampires stood in the central courtyard. Kate turned around on the spot, gazing upwards at the tall walls surrounding them. On this side, within the castle grounds, there were the vestiges of windows at regular intervals, high in the walls, beyond the reach of marauders, but allowing whoever might once have lived there to have some light. The panes were mostly broken, but the mullioned window frames acted as placeholders.

"Kate!" Jackie drew her daughter's attention to the task in hand. "Make sure you hold his one tight – and keep the silver pistol handy." She handed the dog leash to Kate, while Kate held up the pistol again, training it on Victor's heart.

"Although, since you're so ditzy, we could use some help, I think," Jackie said, striding out into the dusty courtyard.

Kate was transfixed, waiting to see what her mother intended next.

When she reached it, Jackie stood in the center of the courtyard, held her hands in the air, looked up into the sky and intoned, "Daemon, esto subjecto voluntati meae. Et ad congregandum eos coram me!"

With a whoosh, and a great draft of wind, two pale, insubstantial demons appeared, taking form before their eyes. Kate took a step back in surprise, and Victor shielded his eyes. These demons were taller than the average human: around seven feet tall, with a reptilian look about them, despite walking on two legs: they had scaly skin, long tails, and claws. However, they were misty in appearance rather than solid, and more ghost-like than Jackie had anticipated. Jackie was somewhat disappointed to see this, but she refused to draw attention to her potential failure in summoning demons. Her strength would only become even greater, and these demons should be sufficient for her purposes at the moment. Besides, she had no time or inclination to worry. They were safe enough here. This was just an additional security measure. Just wait. The best was yet to come.

Meanwhile, since the Nixon women's attention had been solely on the summoning of the demons, William had been able to sprint through the open gates and conceal himself in a doorway off the courtyard. He padded silently up a short, spiral flight of stone steps inside the castle and peered through a narrow arrow slit at those just below him.

30

"We need to keep him here, but out of the way," nodded Jackie. "While we attend to the central matter in hand."

"Okay," Kate said, pointing emphatically with her gun in the direction of the door William had taken to enter the castle himself. Victor trudged off in that direction.

William's blood ran cold as he watched them all – including the two demons, double back from the center of the courtyard, and enter the doorway just beneath him.

***

Attended by the two demons, one on either side of their prisoner, Jackie and Kate led Victor into the Vampire Castle.

"Find any room we can secure," ordered Jackie.

Kate looked momentarily panicked. Judging by the dilapidated state of the building, it seemed unlikely that they would find a lockable door. Besides, would a locked door actually hold the likes of Victor Rothenstein? Even here, in the realm below?

With the barrel of the tiny pistol, she nudged Victor forward through the nearest door. Remarkably, the ancient oak door was blackened but otherwise intact. Stepping into the empty room, Kate looked around. There were only a couple of pieces of furniture in the otherwise empty room, and they looked too raddled with woodworm to be of much use as a weapon or battering ram to break him out of the place. A long, low dark wood bench stood in the middle of the floor, and a long, low cupboard in Old English Tudor style stood against the wall, one door hanging off.

"How do we secure him, Mother?" asked Kate, in concern.

"Leave the demons on guard outside. They will make sure he does not leave," said Jackie. "But come on, now. No more of this. We have work to do."

They left Victor standing in the room, the dog chain still hanging limply from his neck, closing the door behind them. They went down the stone corridor, intending to settle themselves into another of its dusty rooms to plan their next steps.

"What must we do, Mother?" asked Kate, warily testing her weight on an old chair with her hands before tentatively sitting herself down.

Jackie turned around and smiled. It was a smile that even Kate found unnerving. "We start making plans to revive the ancient race of vampires who live here."

"They are still alive?" asked Kate, a bit unsure of herself.

"Of course!" Jackie laughed, throwing her arms wide. "Well… not exactly alive, but definitely undead. They merely await their awakening!"

Kate frowned, still uncertain. "But… how?"

"We must open the 'sleep-lock'!"

Kate didn't know what to say, unwilling to repeat again the word, 'how?' for fear of evoking her mother's irritable wrath. She stood blankly.

Jackie perused her face, waiting in amusement. She bored quickly. "To do that, we need the blood of a newborn human child."

***

Victor stood with his face pressed against one of the arrow slits, his face frozen in horror. Even if he could turn himself into a bat, he couldn't fit through that slim space.

A scuffling sound behind him made him turn around, fast, hissing and ready to attack.

William had swung his legs out of the low cupboard, and was now easing the rest of his body out.

Victor stopped hissing immediately, and stood alert, his ears straining to hear whether or not the demons outside had been alerted by the sound. Nothing.

William stretched himself, his face screwed up in pain. He whispered urgently. "Dammit, Rothenstein. Why am I having to go through this? How come you're allowing yourself to be pussy-whipped like this?"

Rothenstein glared at him, his fangs exposed, itching to bite him, but knowing he couldn't. Victor needed him.

William laughed drily. "Just… yankin' your chain!" And he gave the dog leash around Victor's neck a tiny tug.

Rothenstein seethed, barely able to contain the hiss of outrage. "If I didn't need you – human…" he spat, his hand pointing directly in William's face, then his index finger curled into his fist, threateningly, too.

"Don't forget – I owe you nothing," William said, equally aggressively, although both of them kept their voices low for fear of rousing the demon guards.

"Except your life." Victor fixed him with a stare. "You owe me your life."

They held one another's gaze for several seconds.

"This is getting us nowhere!" Victor turned away, but spun back around almost immediately. "Jackie intends to open the sleep-lock!"

"I don't even know what that means," William said, his concern growing in seeing Victor's distress.

Victor explained. "She wants the vampire legions to be revived. To bring them out of their sleep…"

Will stared at the vampire with suspicion. Why would this bother Rothenstein? He would be in his element, surely?

"But the sleep-lock mustn't be opened," Victor said grimly. "Not by Jackie. She is not an adept. She does not have the relevant experience and arcane knowledge. But her overweening pride and arrogance makes her reckless. She believes she is all-powerful!" William could see the desperation in Victor's eyes. He looked – honestly – appalled and terrified! It chilled William to the bone to see Rothenstein like that.

Victor went on: "If the ritual is not done properly, it will release the Red Beast of Hell!" He swallowed hard, his wild eyes searching William's. "And the red beast can't be controlled by Jackie. Possibly not by anyone…" He slumped down onto the bench.

William found himself placing a hand on Victor's shoulder, encouraging him to continue.

Victor cleared his throat gently, and whispered urgently, "The Red Beast will enter Earth through the Darkness and cause an utter bloodbath. Nothing – and I mean nothing – will survive. Not even vampires."

William took in what Victor had said. He had never seen anyone so terrified, and he could only believe that what the vampire said was true. To see a strong and powerful, cruel creature such as Rothenstein brought to his knees like this was shocking. But that was nothing compared with what he promised, should Jackie take that huge risk for her own gains.

"What can we do?" asked Will, instinctively allying himself again with his enemy. He knew that Rothenstein must have a plan. "Why have you saved me?"

"I needed you to remain human because you must go from here and return to the human world."

William's mind raced. How would he find himself back through that darkness? It had seemed to take hours, maybe even days, as time seemed to not have the same quantum properties in this realm. He had no idea how to get back to the cellar – to the real world again.

As if reading his mind, Victor said dismissively, "Do not trouble yourself with petty fears and worries. With my help, you will find your way. That is the least of your troubles."

"And what is the most of my worries?" asked Will, with suspicion.

"You must go to Herman Thayer's house…"

Will frowned. "Who is that?"

"Herman was a collector of arcane books and artefacts," explained Victor. "He was killed. You need not worry about encountering him. You must look around for a special book, the Grimoire Țepeș."

Will's face was still set in a serious expression of puzzlement.

Victor went on. "The Grimoire Țepeș is the only solution to our current problem. It's an ancient vampire codex diabolis in which Dracula himself describes the spell to control and even destroy the Red Beast, if summoned."

William remained impassive.

"I cannot emphasize enough," Victor said, taking William firmly by the shoulders and speaking directly into his shocked face. "This is our only hope. It must be done."

A million thoughts, worries and concerns sped through William's mind, like a rollercoaster full of loose sheets of paper, scattering everything chaotically across a wide area. If only he could gather his thoughts, he might be able to make some sense of all this. But no.

"Wait," said Victor. Needlessly, Will thought, since he didn't have a clue which way to turn, so he certainly wasn't ready to set off yet.

Victor took his own hand up to his mouth and bit down hard on it. Drawing it away from his lips, Will could see the indentation of his front teeth like a red smile, with two bloody holes where his fangs had sunk in.

"I need to do this for you," Victor said.

Victor pressed his thumb in the blood, and swept it up across William's forehead. Will flinched, but then pulled himself together and kept himself dead still. Victor marked Will's head with an upside-down cross drawn in Victor's own blood.

William felt an odd burning sensation as Victor traced the mark.

"This mark will not be visible to anyone else once our minds are joined."

William simply nodded.

Victor continued. "I need to teach you a vampire communication spell so we can keep in touch," he said, and proceeded to dictate an incantation, inviting William to parrot it back. Will's priestly education had given him a decent background in Latin, so he picked it up quickly and easily.

The moment the words were spoken, William felt as though he had a distinctively split personality. He could sense both his thoughts and Victor's. William knew that he only need to think about Victor Rothenstein and he would personally relive the vampire's memories…all the murders…the eons of lovers…the unquenchable bloodlust of the alpha vampire. He shuddered at the thought. Likewise, he sensed that Victor could see into his memories and most intimate personal life as well. Their darkened minds were telepathically linked.

Pulling away from this odd and nauseating sensation of being mind-raped by evil itself, William shook his head, trying to clear it.

"Now, how the hell do I get out of here?" asked Will, thinking of the demon guards stationed outside.

"I believe she has programmed them to be alert to MY leaving," Victor stated. "And they are transitory beings – not of full strength. I can only account for it by your presence," Victor suggested. "For some reason – possibly the existence of a priest nearby – when Jackie Nixon summoned these demons, she managed to achieve only a mere shadow of the usual power of a demon. They are not exactly – how shall we say? – Intelligent beings. And because she has focused on their sole task as being my containment; their power is limited to that."

William looked doubtful. "Are you sure?"

"One can never be entirely sure," Victor smiled, but it was a wry and apologetic smile; with no malice or deceit. Will raised his eyebrows.

"But, for added assurance, I will cause a distraction," Victor said. "Hide behind the door, and slip out when they come in. The simplest tricks are often the best."

William concealed himself behind the heavy oak door, one arm outstretched to bear the weight of it should the demons burst in through the door and potentially flatten him.

"One very important warning," Victor added, seriously. "It's imperative that no one knows you're still alive."

William nodded.

Stepping into the center of the room, Victor threw himself down on the floor, taking the old bench with him, with a mighty cracking sound as it splintered beneath him, and he cried out in agony.

The door was flung open and the two demons flew in, leaping over to the supine vampire and dragging the moaning and crying Victor up, holding him by his arms.

Meanwhile, as quick as a flash during the disturbance, William slipped quietly out from behind the door, and sprinted down the stairs, across the yard, and out of the huge rusted gate.

Following Victor's psychic guidance like a navigation system, he ran straight through the ultraviolet landscape and didn't stop until he hit the eerie thick blackness beyond.

CHAPTER 2

Police Officer Dwayne Cooley shook his head, his eyes out on stalks, unable to tear them away from the sight of the pale, twisted body at his feet. He was not long out of training, a callow youth whose already pale complexion had turned an alabaster white that made him look barely more alive than the corpse he was looking at. Even his freckles had paled at the sight.

Another construction worker, dead! This time, a few hundred yards outside the restricted fenced-off area, near the almost-completed old Madison house owned by Jackie Nixon. The body of the man lay sprawled under a newly-laid hedge, just outside the property.

"Jesus. Fuck me," he whispered.

"That's a little blasphemous, Cooley," snorted his colleague, Detective Susan Lafitte. She hunkered down beside the dead man and, using two fingers in a pincer movement, she peeled the khaki shirt collar away from his neck.

"Good grief!" she exclaimed, involuntarily. "Shit. It's just like the others."

She had exposed two small, blood-encrusted puncture wounds on the man's throat.

"See?" said Dwayne Cooley, a trembling hand covering his mouth. "Vampires! I told you!"

"Don't be ridiculous!" snapped Susan Lafitte, standing up and fixing Cooley with a stare. "No such thing. It's some weird serial killer, some Goth Emo type. Vampire wannabe, I grant you. But there's no such thing as vampires, so don't even think it. Or say it. And listen up, Cooley. We gotta keep this on the down-low…"

"What d'you mean?" asked Cooley. "We gotta report it in, like the others."

"Of course we do, idiot." Lafitte gave him a look of scorn and disbelief. She wished she hadn't brought this young officer out on such a case, but her usual partner was off work, ill with stress after the murder of the night before. She'd had no choice.

She said emphatically, "But the press gotta hear nothing about the details, you hear?"

"Too late," murmured Cooley, nodding towards a familiar male figure striding across the construction development plot, his iPhone camera trained on the scene.

Lafitte glared. "Shit. That's all we need. Who was supposed to be securing the perimeter?"

It was Augustin Jones, local journalist with the *Clarksburg Exponent Telegram*. As his lean figure approached, it became apparent that he was smiling.

"Who the hell let you in here?" Lafitte snarled, stepping in front of the body to obscure it from view. She was a substantial woman, and made a formidable barrier.

Augustin Jones grinned. "I have my contacts."

"No pictures," Lafitte said, holding one hand up, directly in front of his camera phone's lens. "Print them, and we'll close down the paper. Gonna send you home, too, Gus."

Augustin Jones simply stood there, grinning. "No can do, Officer. The citizens have a right…"

Gathering himself together, Cooley took a couple of strides towards the reporter and grabbed Jones by the shoulders before gently steering him away. "Sorry, but we have to ask you to leave. This is a crime scene, sir, and you are contaminating it!"

"Pah-ha-ha!" Augustin Jones burst out laughing. "Coolio, boy—you sound like you've been watching cop shows again. Come on! It's not like you haven't been trampling all over the evidence yourselves, like a couple of hicks. Besides, the public needs to know the facts. Come on! Give me something. It's another vampire murder, isn't it?"

Cooley's firm grip wavered, and he looked uneasily at Susan Lafitte's grim expression.

A knowing smile crept across Jones's face. "It is!" His look was triumphant. "Isn't it? A vampire murder!"

***

A number of strange occurrences had taken place in the last few days, in and around the fire and flood-ravaged town of Melas that was now in the process of redevelopment, and had already been partially reconstructed with Nixon money. Since buying the ruins of the town and since the death of her wealthy husband, Jackie Nixon had been able to invest more and more in the new developments. This mission was ostensibly for the benefit of the community, but truly, Jackie's major motivation was the immense supernatural power in the site of the town of Melas itself. In addition, Jackie had personally and professionally—if not demonically—invested in the old Madison residence, which she intended to live in herself. And the construction workers had unwittingly used the soul-stones and human bone-ash that Jackie had explicitly requested be incorporated into the body of the building itself. Once the house was completed—which it was, apart from furnishings and decoration—Jackie had been able to perform and arcane ritual in its cellar and utilize the house's power to open up the portal to the Darkness.

Since then, the killings had started happening amongst the construction company workers onsite in Melas. It had started with the death of one of the security staff assigned to patrolling the perimeter fence. Both this man and the German Shepherd dog that accompanied him had been found with their throats ripped open, and all blood apparently lost. It had been difficult to establish exactly what had happened—there were some signs of a struggle, and the throats of both human and animal looked to have been slashed jaggedly with an unknown weapon. Or, it could have been that a wild animal—like a bear, or bears—had killed both. Strangely enough, the blood found at the scene, where the bodies lay, was negligible. There was hardly any there.

"Must have been killed elsewhere, and the bodies dumped here," Susan Lafitte had said, after arriving on the scene and surveying the surroundings.

It was strange. It was shocking. But it was, at least, a one-off. Still, security had been increased, and the guards patrolled in pairs.

The second night that something uncannily similar happened, it was, naturally, even more suspicious. One of the construction managers, who had returned to the site after dark, had been found dead. Susan Lafitte's usual partner, John Savage, had taken one look and freaked out. It was his brother. She had sent him home immediately.

During the evening before, Dave Savage had reportedly cheerily hailed the pair of security guards on patrol, explaining why he was there, and then let himself into the locked complex surrounding the secured and dangerous parts of the site under construction, driving through the gate to the site office.

"He forgot his phone," Donovan Smith, the construction site's chief manager said vaguely, looking down at his employee's cell phone in his own hand, in bewilderment.

The security guards had found the body in the early hours of the morning, deathly white and bloodless. After calling the police, they had rung Don immediately and he had arrived soon afterwards.

Ever since then, he had been itching to ask the officers a particular question, but it had seemed churlish, given the reason the police had arrived. There was a man dead, after all. A man he knew. But like a persistent nagging in his brain, after an hour or so, Don could resist no longer.

"Look. Sorry to ask right now, but do you know…" Don began, "…has any progress been made on finding my wife?"

Susan Lafitte frowned at him. "Sir. I'm afraid I don't know. You'll have to speak to the officer dealing with that."

"Right. Sorry."

This couple of strange and deadly events did not help Don's own anxiety about his wife, Alison, who had apparently disappeared. He had reported her to the police as a missing person, and by now, he hadn't seen her for a couple of days. He was troubled for two reasons. One, it was most unlike Alison to go missing. Two, although it seemed impossible to conceive the thought, she might have discovered that he had been having an affair with Jackie Nixon herself. His guilt had been eating away at him, but he felt trapped. Jackie Nixon, after all, was tremendously wealthy, and the future of his construction company depended on this big Melas contract. But where was Alison?

Unbeknown to Don Smith, Alison had entered Jackie Nixon's new house in Melas, and had never left.

Police had cordoned off the route into the fenced-off piece of development land where the construction manager had been found, lying beside his vehicle. Dave Savage clearly hadn't even made it inside the metal hut that formed the site office to collect his phone. He hadn't even opened up the small building. His door keys were still in his hand, the car door wide open, and the cell phone he had intended to pick up there was still lying on the table in the locked hut, where Don had found it later.

Upon being interviewed by the police about the victim's last known actions, one of the guards stated, "He told us he was locking the gate behind him, so he would be 'safe as... safe as houses', he said."

The other security guy confirmed, "That was the last we saw of him. But we presumed he'd left by the time we got back to the gate. Takes a good hour for us to walk the whole perimeter. Should've only taken him five minutes to get his phone."

The gashes in this particular man's neck were less frenzied; more distinct. Two definite, smaller rips in the skin of his throat, less than two inches apart.

"Looks like someone took a knife, tried to make it look like a vampire bite," said Detective Lafitte. "Sick fucks."

But one major thing troubled her: where was the blood?

Even though Susan Lafitte had a terrible feeling about this, she could only assume that again, the man had been killed elsewhere, and the body dumped. But so far, they had not located the seven or eight pints of blood that must have pooled somewhere, soaking into the earth. The perimeter fence was still locked, surrounding the as-yet undeveloped land, to protect the piles of bricks and valuable building materials, vehicles and equipment. Somehow, someone had managed to penetrate the secure area, and either locked the gate behind themselves, or found another way in. It was weird, but not impossible.

The police were still waiting for autopsy results from the county coroner, but from the blue-gray pallor of the bodies and the lack of blood at the scene, it looked like they had died from exsanguination. Whilst the savagely gashed necks in the first murder case accounted for the loss of blood, as far as she could tell, Susan Lafitte just couldn't account for the smallness of the puncture wounds and the lack of blood in this second case. Sure, an artery had probably been hit, which would mean considerable blood-loss through spray, but unless someone had been hanging them upside down to drain their blood, how could it have all disappeared completely, from such tiny wounds? And, moreover, where was it?

**

Up to this point, the police had managed to keep the details of the murders to themselves, releasing very few facts to the media. Yes, two people had been murdered. And a dog. Within days of one another. Within a quarter mile of one another.

"Second Melas Stabbing!" read the headlines. All other details of the nature of the killing, and the method employed, were kept confidential. The police needed to keep some things to themselves.

But Melas was a small town surrounded by small towns full of people with a small-town mentality. Everyone knew one another. Security guards had friends and families, as did cops and construction workers. Word must have got out.

And now, there was this third murder, in the same vicinity. Three times is a charm, they say.

By the time Augustin Jones had gone back to the offices of the *Exponent Telegram* and performed his magic, the next evening's front page shouted: "Melas Vampire Murders!"

In addition, a number of women had gone missing recently. Two, in addition to Donovan Smith's wife. They had apparently vanished without a trace. But it was early days yet for missing persons. Grown women who had been missing for a day or two didn't make headlines. Yet. Not when there were people having their throats ripped out on a nightly basis.

Coincidentally, these strange murder developments or phenomena had started to occur at exactly the same time as Jackie Nixon and her daughter, Kate, had begun enjoying their new vampiric powers.

In fact, they were unstoppably driven by their vampiric powers.

Each night, the two newborn female vampires left the Darkness. They had no choice but to do it. This was a necessary action, since, as far as the two new vampires were aware, no humans existed there in the Darkness. And they needed human blood to survive. Now dead, and yet undead, they experienced a raging hunger and a rampant thirst—an extreme craving—that no ordinary food or drink could satisfy.

They needed no teaching from their mentor and prisoner, the vampire of hundreds of years' standing, Victor Rothenstein, since what they felt was instinctive. Although it was forever dark in the Darkness, their bodies were acclimatized to the circadian rhythms and the passage of time from the land and the lives they had left. So when darkness fell in Melas, the stirring of their vampire lusts and instincts affected them strongly. It was a yearning that drew them like a magnet; like an

47

arrow powered from a crossbow, seeking its target with its sharp bite.

With a thrill of excitement and a preternatural urge that was irresistible, and with a mere flicker of thought and intention, their bodies transformed within the blink of an eye into gigantic, black bat creatures, and with a swoop of leathery wings, they flew through the Darkness, and through the portal into the live world, and out into Melas, seeking their prey.

Crazed by an uncontrollable blood-lust and inexperienced in attacking humans and satisfying their hunger, on that first night, they had focussed their attention on the first person they saw—the security guard—and his dog. With a psychic understanding that passed between mother and daughter, Kate instinctively understood that she must take out the dog, while her mother concentrated on the human. They both struck at once, their massive wings flapping down from the sky, leaving the guard paralyzed, awestruck and amazed, while the dog barked only once before Kate ripped out its throat and drained its blood like a good-time girl chugging a creamy cocktail. The first night, by their own admission, they didn't know what they were doing. They were savage and inept, tearing great chunks out of the flesh of both man and beast.

When her mother, Jackie, had taken her fill of the security guard's warm blood, she had passed his limp body on to Kate. The younger woman plunged her lips into the moist, open gash of his throat and sucked hard, since Jackie had taken the first effortless pumping spurts into her own mouth and drank it down while the man's heart was still beating the blood through his body. Kate had a more difficult job to do, sucking hard like a child at a straw at the bottom of a milkshake.

But a vampire has to feed. And they were conscious that, in holding Victor Rothenstein prisoner in the Darkness, they were depriving him of his opportunity to sustain himself.

"I wouldn't care," sneered Jackie, wiping the security guard's blood from her mouth with a delicate silk handkerchief, "But I do still need the old bastard and his skills and knowledge."

Kate shrugged. "What do we do? Let him go? Bring him out with us, chained to us?"

This was all new to her, and despite her own sharpness and intelligence, Kate had no real idea of the practicalities of being a vampire. Her mother had at least studied the arcane arts for over forty years, since she was a small child herself, brought up by her father, the occultist Walter Pinkman, friend and associate of Victor Rothenstein.

Jackie shot her daughter a knowing look. "We must do what the lioness does." Kate frowned. So her mother explained, "Go hunting, while the male lion lazes around. We need to bring the meal home for him. Get a take-out."

"Take a body to Victor?" asked Kate. "Save him some blood?"

"No. We need to satiate ourselves. First, we drink the blood of our own victims," warned Jackie. "Then, we find him a live one of his own. We must not kill the prey we find for Victor. We must only render them unconscious."

"Do you mean… just drink enough of their blood to make them faint?" asked Kate, in her naivety.

Jackie hissed loudly, her fangs exposed. "No, fool! That would just 'turn' them! We need them human, and still alive! If we give the vampire's kiss to just anybody, we will be overrun with foolish new vampires, and that still will not feed the old goat in our castle." Jackie's face twisted deviously. "There is a whole city of ancient vampires beneath the castle that are only waiting to do my bidding." She gestured dramatically, sweeping one hand to the sky and holding it in the air. "But only when I have brought them to life!"

She brought her hand down into a fist and said, emphatically, "But for that to happen, I still need Victor Rothenstein. Alive… as far as a vampire can be alive. And well. Therefore, he needs us to bring him fresh blood."

Kate nodded. "Then we find someone easy to overwhelm, and—just for kicks—I say we take him a woman."

Jackie arched one eyebrow. "Well, that is his proclivity. I suppose we need to keep him sweet. Why not?"

That first night, when the news of murder hadn't reached the public, they had found it quite easy to identify a suitable person as they soared across the surrounding area in their bat-forms, and they swiftly targeted a woman walking alone that night. She didn't know what had hit her when the two voracious beasts of the night air swept down at the speed of light and subdued her by some gentle pressure on the nerve in her neck, before carrying her off.

Flying across the dark sky, the distance between where they had picked up the woman and Jackie's house, where the portal stood in the cellar was no distance at all. Once they were in the Darkness, it was only a matter of minutes, a few beats of their huge black wings, before they reached the eerie purple light of the castle.

Grinning, Kate and Jackie dropped the unconscious woman at Victor Rothenstein's feet.

"A redhead," he said, amused by their delight. "My favorite!"

The woman moaned and stirred. But before she had a chance to even open her eyes, Rothenstein dipped to the ground and sank her feet into the woman's neck. Her eyelids fluttered a little, then her blue eyes opened wide in shock, her mouth forming an 'O' of surprise.

Victor pressed her body close to his, and sucked at her throat. The woman's eyes closed, and she moaned again, this time as if in ecstasy. They could hear a squelching, rhythmical gush and sucking sound. The woman threw back her head and gave a long, low, orgasmic groan, then panted heavily.

Kate felt a pulsing feeling in her vagina, her inner lips involuntarily throbbing in excitement. She looked uneasily at her mother, who stood transfixed, staring at Victor, her eyes wide, her tongue licking from the corner of her mouth, across her upper lip, lasciviously. She was obviously turned on, too.

Well, this is embarrassing, thought Kate.

Victor cupped the woman's face in his hands lovingly, then a sharp 'crack!' broke the silence as he snapped her neck without a second's thought.

Kate and Jackie looked at one another.

"See?" Jackie taunted him. "You're really no better than us. You're as evil as shit!"

Victor shrugged. "Never said I was holier than thou."

They looked down at the dead body on the floor of the room that was Victor's prison.

"Hmmm. And I suppose we'll have to get another one for you tomorrow," Jackie said, sarcastically. She stood with her hand on her hips and struck a pose, cocking one hip.

"I could make it easier for you at feeding time, if you would only let me go," Victor suggested.

Jackie shrieked with laughter. "Do you think I am an idiot?"

"I'll come back," Victor wheedled. "I know I am tied to you in servitude, oh, queen!"

Jackie looked at him askance, trying to make out if she could detect a note of sarcasm in his tone of voice.

"Please," Victor said, trying to restrain his desperation. "It makes sense. Otherwise, doesn't it seem like you're *my* servant, hunting for me, fetching me food? Is that a task worthy of a queen?"

Jackie scowled, her eyes flashing anger. "How dare you insinuate that?"

"Please," he persisted, hastily changing his tone to one that was more subservient. "Let me go, and you'll see how I will serve *you*. As you deserve."

Jackie firmly held up her hand. "Shut up, Rothenstein. My answer is 'no'. I'm not falling for your cunning wiles. Kate—we're going."

Kate, her eyes still wide, wondering at the exchange, followed her mother out of the door, which was hastily shut and guarded by the pale demons outside.

Jackie was marching up the corridor, her shoulders set, by the time Kate got outside the room. She had to run after Jackie to catch up with her.

"What's the matter, Mother?" she said, panting, as she got within arm's reach of her advancing back. "We have Victor under control. I think what he says makes sense. We could easily get him…"

"No!" Jackie interrupted, her voice ringing off the castle's cold stone walls. She swung round to face her daughter, with blazing eyes glaring into hers. "I don't trust him."

"But we have to, don't we? To an extent? He's been helpful so far, telling us the secrets of this castle…"

"I'm certain he knows many secrets about this realm that he's not sharing with us," Jackie said bitterly. "And I'm not letting him out of this castle, until we know everything. Until I have awakened the vampires of this ancient city and am truly Queen!"

"So… that means we do have to hunt for him to keep him 'alive'…" Kate muttered.

"There's no rest for the undead."

They resigned themselves to their task.

Now no one was safe in the towns surrounding Melas anymore. Jackie and Kate attacked any men near the construction site for themselves and their own bloodlust. But so far, all that was known by the police and the media was that some men had been killed. Missing women were not a cause for concern until a day or two had gone by, since no bodies were found.

During subsequent nights, after word had got around the Melas area about the killings, and women were more cautious—setting their own self-inflicted night-time curfew, the two female vampires found they had to travel a little further afield for Victor's particular prey.

Jackie and Kate consequently took several unconscious women back to Victor, who drank their blood, then instantly snapped their necks. He tried a different tack each night in an attempt to persuade Jackie to let him go, but she remained unmoved.

"Is this feminism?" he sneered, in one attempt to attack her female pride, taunting her in order to draw her into releasing him. "Would a powerful woman be a slave to a man?"

"You're not a man in any sense of the word," Jackie retorted, before flouncing out.

Then, another time, he tried flattery and obsequiousness. "Your Highness, all-powerful lady of the night—I only wish to do your bidding. Please allow me to serve you, to feed you, to prostrate myself at your feet with my humble offerings."

"Lady of the night?" Jackie coughed, barely able to contain her amusement. "Is that how you praise me? By calling me a whore?"

No matter what Victor tried, it was all to no avail.

***

Donovan Smith, meanwhile, exasperated by the lack of police progress, was looking for his wife, Alison.

CHAPTER 3

Jackie Nixon stood at the castle window, her palms flat on the stone mullioned window frame, looking out through the ancient mottled glass. Her blank gaze was trained on the edge of the eerie purple light that enshrouded them, straining to see into the palpable darkness beyond.

Jackie and Kate were keen to know what it held. Beyond the shimmering purple hue that hung over the vampire castle like a pall, all they knew was the density of the black velvet atmosphere they had walked through when they first arrived.

There was much still to do. Jackie had so much to learn – and Victor was the only one who could help her, regardless of how much the thought rankled her. The Darkness held many secrets, Jackie was sure, and she hungered to know them; but she did not trust Victor Rothenstein to freely show her. She needed some assurance that he would not escape from her grasp, because she required the arcane knowledge he held to enable her to safely revive the legions of vampires who slept in the lost city surrounding and beneath the castle. In an ideal world, the demon guards would ensure that he was kept tightly locked within the castle room until the appropriate time came for the sacred ritual that would awaken her vampire hordes, who would, naturally, obey their queen. And yet, Victor was also the most valuable guide to the Darkness available to her. She ground her teeth in frustration, grimacing as she did so, and pressed her hot forehead against the cold glass of the window.

Jackie needed Victor more than she could bear to admit.

There was nothing else for it. She had decided that she would have to take him to guide her in their exploration through the Darkness, rather than keep him prisoner at the castle. But the pale, gray-skinned demon guards would accompany them, and Victor would be held securely throughout.

"Come, Kate!"

She swept out of the room, her daughter trailing behind her.

Victor, as usual, was seething with resentment when the heavy lock opened on the door of his jail-room, and a demon guard stepped forward, and bowed, holding the heavy door open for Jackie to make a grand entrance.

Victor was no fashionista himself, but he could certainly see that Jackie had made an effort with her attire. She wore a long, close-fitting purple silk sheath dress with a plunging neckline, emphasising her ample cleavage. She had apparently dyed her hair a striking blue-black, which only emphasized the paleness of her face, the purple lipstick and the striking black eye makeup she wore giving her the appearance of an Egyptian queen -- a Cleopatra. She wore a tumble of raven curls piled on top of her head, the hairpiece held in place with an extravagant peacock feather fascinator.

It was all Victor could do to stop himself from sneering. "Well! Aren't we quite the Vampire Queen?"

To this ancient male vampire, she lacked sophistication. She was merely a cartoonish caricature of a vampire queen. Simply a pale impersonation, some feeble attempt to portray a fictional character in a movie based on an Anne Rice novel. A wannabe. An Addams Family Morticia.

You disappoint me, Jackie, he thought to himself. *I expected better of you. In the human world, you were a wealthy intelligent woman of some taste. But this pseudo-power has turned your megalomaniac head.*

Jackie stared Victor out, one eyebrow cocked mockingly at him.

Behind her, dressed in a modest black gown, stood Kate, like a shadow of her extravagantly showy mother. Her blonde hair was slicked back with some kind of gel that made it look darker, and her pale skin looked pinched and tired. She averted her eyes to the floor.

Jackie announced, "So, Victor… I have decided that I will permit you to leave the castle…"

Involuntarily, Victor's eyebrows arched in surprise, his eyes hungry with excitement.

"…on condition…" Jackie warned, raising one black-polished fingernail like a talon. "… that you submit to me entirely. Guards! Clip on the collar."

Victor seethed, as a hulking, scaly gray guard stepped forward, the vicious studded dog-collar in his bony hands. The old vampire's eyes flashed hatred and humiliation, but he kept his mouth shut. He did not trust himself to speak, so eaten away by suppressed hatred was he. He had no doubt that Jackie was aware of his feelings towards her on this matter, but he needed to regain her trust. If he were ever to be free again, he had to ingratiate himself with this self-styled queen of the vampires. And wait for his human ally, William, to give him an opportunity to rise to his former state.

And so, Victor once again allowed himself to be led by the neck, one end of a dog leash in Jackie's elegant hands. Either side of him walked a large, muscular, reptilian guard covered in gray scales like a long-dead fish, their red eyes glowing in the purple light.

His head held high despite his abasement, Victor strode out of his prison as best he could, following the swishing long skirts of his powerful mistress. Without wanting to, he found his eyes straying to her voluptuous figure, from the tightly cinched waist to her silken ass, and his stare fixed on Jackie's swaying hips, which were almost hypnotic in their rhythmical, fluid movement.

Damn the woman! he said to himself; then almost laughed. They were all damned, after all.

***

Outside the castle walls, the eerie purple light that was focused on the castle only highlighted part of the desolate wasteland outside, permeating the Darkness for a few hundred yards. Beyond that, Jackie and Kate could see nothing but black.

"I would have you show me around the Vampire City on another occasion, Victor," Jackie said as they walked, casting her gaze across the purple landscape, where only grassy mounds and mossy rubble indicated the remnants of the once-mighty Vampire City that had been destroyed.

"There is little to see, Your Highness, except what you can see now. It was razed to the ground."

"But below the ground…" Jackie said archly. "That is where my interest lies."

"The Vampire Cemetery," Victor confirmed. "Of course."

"I should like to see where my subjects rest and my troops lie. And from where they will arise again."

Victor merely nodded.

Jackie appraised him, reading his hesitation correctly. She added, "When the time is right."

"Indeed, Your Highness."

The small procession of figures, walking in silence, reached the boundary where the Darkness began, and they stopped.

Jackie, still holding up his leash with her fingertips, as if she were afraid to touch anything so dirty, turned to Victor, and tugged sharply on his chain.

Victor struggled to conceal the sneer of disgust on his lips.

"Madam?" he said, with dignity.

"Your Highness," she corrected, jerking the leash again harshly, causing the cruel barbs inside the collar to penetrate his neck. It was nothing like the bite that had converted him so many centuries ago: thrilling and exhilarating – offering eternal life. This was momentarily painful, and lastingly degrading.

"Highness," he hissed, in an obsequious tone.

"You will escort me around the Darkness, Victor," Jackie smiled. "With your own escorts close by, of course." She passed the leash to one of the pale gray demon guards. "I'm bored. Entertain me."

The act of her leading Victor by the throat had been more ritualistic and ceremonial than practical and purposeful. She had wanted to demonstrate that she was his mistress, and now, she had tired of the game.

Victor, his head held high, spoke. "Your Highness, if I am to lead the way – I am restrained by whoever holds me back, which makes it impossible. Therefore, may I suggest that I am at least temporarily unleashed, to facilitate our speedier progress?"

Jackie stared at him steadily, the last of the purple light gleaming intensely on her purple gown so that it looked almost fluorescent. Her pale skin was bathed in lilac light; her eyes, inscrutable.

"He has a point, Mother," said Kate. "Hasn't he been punished enough? I think he knows his place."

Jackie turned her gaze on her daughter. "I should hope he does." She paused, appraisingly. "Very well. Unhook the chain and remove the collar," she ordered one of the two guards. "Stay next to him at all times. But any funny business, Rothenstein, and these guards will have no hesitation in destroying you."

"Very well, Your Highness," Victor said, lifting his chin while the guard released him from the collar. Once freed, he bowed low, allowing himself a broad, private grin while his head was dipped, which he adjusted to a sincere, respectful expression as soon as he stood up and his face was visible again.

"Advance, then, Victor, and show me all you know," Jackie said.

Victor nodded. "Your Highness. Princess. After you." He swept his hand across into the Darkness, and all five of them stepped forward into the Darkness.

***

That cloying, thick, black velvet feeling always alarmed Kate. She breathed it in, trying to settle her racing heart. She and her mother had flown through the Darkness as bats on numerous occasions for their hunting expeditions, and that was bad enough. Even though they flew as fast as they could, the dense air resisted their leathery wings far more than the fresh earthly air outside in the human world. When they had first proceeded through the Darkness to arrive at the castle, she had been too new a vampire, too afraid. But now it was time to familiarise herself.

Victor's voice rang clear and close by, through the Darkness. "May I… instruct the guards to illuminate us, Your Highness?"

"I suppose so," Jackie said, feeling slightly uneasy at the advantages she had already given Victor.

Instantaneously, there was light. Kate blinked, trying to adjust her eyes to the shocking brightness. On either side of Victor, the guards held flaming torches that had suddenly burst forth with a yellowish-orange glow. The fire in them crackled, and as their eyes became accustomed to the duskiness beyond the small pools of amber light, they could make out muted shapes emerging from the darkness surrounding them. Muffled moans were just distinguishable through the thick black fog, too. Kate had heard these before, but they still unsettled her. To Jackie, however, they were mildly thrilling. They gave her a frisson that was almost erotic.

"Just over there," said Victor, "is the Sea of Souls."

Jackie nodded rapidly, as if she knew what he was talking about, but she asked, "Which is?"

"Some call it Purgatory," Victor said. "Some call it Hell. It's all a matter of perspective. To me, it's a transitional area – a waiting room, you might say. A place in between journeys. In between destinations."

"You're talking in riddles, Rothenstein. Explain yourself," Jackie said tightly. "For the sake of my daughter."

She hates to feel ignorant, smiled Victor to himself. *But I could benefit from her arrogance.*

"Of course, Your Highness." Victor nodded sharply, in almost a bow. He turned to Kate. "To build into the foundations of her house on the earth plane, your mother has been collecting soul stones – the solid form of human souls. To an extent, it didn't matter whether these souls were good or bad – just as long as they were souls."

"Are you calling me undiscriminating, Victor?" Jackie challenged, one eyebrow arched.

"Not at all, Your Highness. For the purpose of creating a portal to this realm, the distinction is relevant. Human souls were all that was required – in solid form.

"The Sea of Souls…" Victor swept his hand across the horizon, indicating the Darkness and allowed a few seconds to pass for them to drink in the sight. Or the lack of sight, since all was black. "… is an amorphous mass of the souls of the dead. You might call it fluid – in liquid form, as it were. They are those souls who are lost, because they have committed some evil, even if merely some petty wickedness or selfishness in the world. Not sufficient to be sent straight into Hell, you understand. That is too good for them – they are not worthy to serve our Lord and Master, Satan."

He paused for breath again. "First, they must suffer what is called the Torment of Unknowing. They must contemplate their lives, ponder upon their sins, and yet, they still do not know what the resolution will be. Will they go to Heaven? Or to Hell? And that is their exquisite torture," And here, Victor licked his lips lasciviously in satisfaction. "And they do not know for how long they will experience this suffering. It may last forever, or it may last for months or years. Time is meaningless here."

Jackie's eyes gleamed in the torchlight, a lustful smile playing on her purple lips. Those groans were music to her ears, and she took an almost orgasmic pleasure in being here, so close to the guttural sounds of suffering.

But as for her daughter – the haunting, distant howls of tormented souls discomforted Kate.

What's wrong with me? she wondered. *I should feel the same delight as Mom and Victor.*

Involuntarily, she pressed her hand to her abdomen, feeling sick to the stomach.

I'm not a very good vampire at all. Maybe it's because I was the last to be 'turned'. Maybe my transition hasn't fully completed yet, and it needs more time.

She didn't dare mention her doubts to her mother or to Victor. They might think her weak. Perhaps she was.

63

Instead, she had tried to brave it out and be the vampire she ought to be. But there was something not quite right. She couldn't put her finger on it.

"Can we venture further in?" Jackie said eagerly. "I would love to see. Take us there."

"Of course," Victor agreed. "Follow me. But stick together. Especially you, Princess. Some of these lost souls are desperate, and dangerous."

Victor's comment rankled with Kate. It was as if he had read her mind, or felt her vulnerability. Was it *that* obvious that she didn't know what she was doing? That she didn't feel altogether vampiric, despite the evidence to the contrary? After all, she had been bitten. She had fed on blood, on many occasions. She could turn herself into a bat in the blink of an eye, and fly to hunt prey, walking between worlds. To all intents and purposes, she was a vampire.

Then why did she feel this residual sense of 'humanity'?

She could not account for it.

As they stepped further into the thick miasma of the Darkness, the vague forms they had first seen appearing before them like blurred shadows became more defined, and the moans and howls became louder. A dark mass ahead of them was distinguishing itself, developing a humanoid shape, and the solid blackness was shaping itself into features of light and dark shadow.

A couple of paces further in, Kate stopped dead, appalled.

"Behold!" Victor said. "A sinner whose vicious gossip made people miserable."

The flickering flames of the guards' torches cast a trembling circle of light on the hunched figure ahead of them. It wore a shapeless sackcloth robe and its gender was not obvious, but Kate had a sense that it was a woman, although it was grotesquely large, even taller and broader than most men. Lank, greasy ropes of hair hung down, shielding its downturned face. Above it, a demon was steadily whipping its back, while an angelic creature whispered urgently in its ear.

The miserable, hunched-over beast was whimpering softly at first, making the sounds of a snuffling wild animal, but as the group approached, and the light fell on its bulk, it raised its horrifically ugly head, its small black eyes screwed up against the light and barely visible, embedded as they were within the ghastly creases of drooping eyelids and the dry folds of wrinkled yellow skin surrounding its eyes. The remains of a spindly nose, the end rotted away, leaving a ghastly gaping hole fringed with green shreds of skin, was not even the worst of it.

Suddenly, it threw back its head, opening an oversized mouth which seemed to unhinge itself at the jawline, flipping back the entirety of its skull on its neck, exposing not only row after row of small savage shark-like teeth, but a ragged, torn tongue and a bloody, raw-tendoned throat, red and pulsating with a pile of wriggling worms and infected maggots. At the same time, a terrible stench of rotting flesh hit them, and a high-pitched, blood-curdling roar of pain turned Kate's legs to water.

"Oh, my God!" cried Kate, covering her mouth and swallowing down the rush of bile that threatened to escape her throat. She had to turn her head away.

"Do not blaspheme, Princess," Victor said mildly. "Please."

Jackie raised an eyebrow. "I'm impressed!" she said. "If this is how the petty sinners look, and are treated, I can't wait to see the really evil."

"Then you can't wait to see Hell," smiled Victor.

A cacophony of wails, screeches and moans surrounded them in the thick blackness, although slightly muffled by the atmosphere. No other figures were visible because the Darkness was too dense. This terrifying creature before them was trapped forever here, caught in the orange circle of light like an insect suspended in amber.

"I'm surprised to see *that*!" Jackie pointed one long black-painted index-fingernail towards the angelic being. "That isn't an angel, is it? What's going on?"

Victor held up one hand in the gesture of a theatrical comment made aside, the back of his first finger close to the corner of his lips, speaking in a low voice. "One part of the Torment of Unknowing is living in hope. This is not an angel, but a creature of our Master's creation, designed to seduce the mind. If you were to step close enough, you would hear that this 'angel' as you call it, is offering a vision of what might have been. But their raised hopes are dashed, constantly. That's the joy of it, for us. They need to know what they have lost, as well as the pain. That, Your Highness, is the thrilling delight of it all. Listen!"

66

Victor held out his hand, and it was as if this gesture served to amplify the angel-being's words, because they were transmitted clearly into their minds, to the exclusion of all the moaning and crying in their real context.

"To think that God would have saved you!" the angel mocked. "To think that you might have had peace of mind, and respite, had your vicious tongue not caused such distress."

The angel looked the part – a beatific, beautiful face; a flowing white silk gown, and soft, iridescent, feathered wings. Her tone was gentle and soothing, but a note of sarcasm tinged her words.

"Ah, what bliss it would be, to rest in peace," she cooed. "Imagine that… all softness and gentleness. Do you think God will save you? Could there be a slim chance? Yes? No?"

All the while, the horrific creature she spoke to whimpered and the demon behind the gossip's back whipped on, relentlessly. After the gossip's flip-topped skull had surveyed the fury of the demon for a minute or two, its horrific vision upside down, the skull tipped forward again with a soft crash and a gurgling sound as raw wounded flesh hit soft-tissue, bone and teeth.

Kate swallowed hard.

"Onwards?" smiled Victor. "Would you like to see more of these souls?"

"We get the idea," said Kate, clearly her throat and trying to sound authoritative, despite her trembling lips. "What else is there to see?"

"More of the same," shrugged Victor. "Although, if we fly through the Darkness, we can see more, faster."

67

"No!" snapped Jackie. There was no way she was going to give Victor the freedom of his wings. That might be the last she saw of him. "Show us on foot."

"How very old-fashioned, and… human…" said Victor, gently and teasingly, careful not to anger Jackie.

"Well, that's just the kind of vampire queen I am," Jackie retorted with a sneer. She still couldn't make out whether or not Victor had a witty sense of humor, or whether the barbs were meant to hurt her.

Victor said softly, "I wouldn't have you any other way."

"I won't let you *have* me at all, Rothenstein!" Jackie laughed.

Victor gave a gracious bow. "Naturally. I am not worthy."

What he really thought was, *Over your dead body.* But his eyes said, *I love you.*

Jackie looked at him oddly again, and he gazed at her, imagining he was looking at a sexy, attractive woman. Which she certainly was, on the outside, at least. He summoned up all his acting skills to compose his expression to suggest that he was in love with her, but too cool to show how much he adored her. It was a fine line to tread, but he had had centuries of practice in seducing women – human and otherwise.

Jackie looked back at his handsome features, and spotted a fond twinkle in his eye, to her surprise. She did a double-take. Victor had tried so many approaches to gain her trust, and she wasn't a woman to be duped. But she was taken aback to see that there was an almost reticent loving interest in his eyes that appeared to be sincere. She decided that she was warming to him.

"Onwards!" Jackie said, waving her hand dismissively. She had no time for such thoughts. She had an empire to build.

They walked through the Sea of Souls briskly, the torches held aloft by the demon guards occasionally picking out the looming faces of tortured souls, whose haunted eyes – if they had them at all – gazed beseechingly at their high-ranking visitors, hoping for respite or protection.

Kate had lost count of the number of lost souls, and the number of demons and demonic angels they had passed. And there must be many thousands more lost to their sight and hearing.

"It is impossible to ascertain the full extent of the distance or area of the Darkness," Victor explained. "Just as time is meaningless – so, too, is distance. Eternity and infinity are held in the palm of your hand… Your Highness," Victor added, in a sudden flash of inspiration.

Jackie beamed. *I hold infinity and eternity in the palm of my hand!*

The poetry of his words moved her deeply. She loved the idea of that power, and it filled her with a shockingly deep satisfaction. It would have warmed her soul, if she'd had one.

As they got closer to the portal to the earth realm, which led through to the cellar of Jackie's house, Victor stopped. "You will notice that the air is denser here. The veil is thickening, and the capacity of soul power is solidifying. After all, we are approaching the soul-stones which form the foundation of the old Madison house – your present home, Jack… Your Highness."

Jackie's lip twitched to suppress a smile. She even let his familiarity go by without a reprimand. She might not succumb completely to Victor's charms, after all, but if he had some stirrings of... whatever emotion – lust? Love? Respect? – for her at all, if she encouraged it, it would all add to her arsenal of weapons. She needed Victor onside. She needed him, and his knowledge, if she was to awaken the Vampire Army and take over the world. She allowed a momentary vision of that goal, which stirred her to action.

Her mind was suddenly tiring of the Darkness. She had more things to do if she were to achieve her ambitions.

"Yes, we have been here many times," said Jackie, distractedly. "All right. Guards, you may escort Rothenstein back to the castle, and maintain your containment of him."

"What?" Victor was bewildered. Things had been going so well! And here she was, dismissing him! He suddenly felt like a plaything being summarily discarded by a bored child.

Jackie snapped out of her trance and turned on the charm. "Oh, thank you so much, Victor," she gushed. "I am so sorry not to spend more time with you. Unfortunately, I have suddenly remembered something I need to attend to in the other realm."

She pressed her hand on Victor's forearm and leaned in closer to speak huskily to him, her hot breath moistening the hollows inside his ear.

"We must spend more time together, Victor. Wait for me, my dear," she almost groaned, as if with desire.

Against his better judgment and to his great surprise, this physical and verbal intimacy caused his cock to twitch to attention.

Kate, meanwhile, had spent most of the time trying to desensitise herself from her surroundings. For some reason, the cries of the not-yet damned affected Kate even more than the first time they had walked through, when Victor had initially taken them to the castle. She felt somehow more emotional now than when she was first 'turned'.

Maybe my period is due, she said to herself. *But – do vampires even have periods?*

That was another question she didn't feel comfortable asking anyone.

On second thoughts, she decided that they probably didn't. Her period was already overdue. She guessed that the early menopause must be one of the hazards of being undead.

CHAPTER 4

William looked in the mirror of the motel bathroom, taking in his exhausted, red-rimmed eyes. He lifted the heavy fringe of hair off his forehead, exposing the brown upside-down cross of dried blood still encrusted on his brow.

He didn't know if he still *had* to keep it or not. He didn't know whether it was this image that had actually given him the power – if it *was* the power in itself, or if it simply *symbolized* the power and was only part of the ritual that had enabled him to get back safely to the human world. The communication spell had worked, hadn't it? *Although I haven't heard from Victor for many hours, now!* Maybe this blood symbol was only part of that. Maybe he would retain the telepathic power and apparent invincibility against evil, even if he washed of the grotesque anomaly on his forehead.

As an ex-priest, this Satanic symbol didn't sit well with Will at all. It was blasphemous. Sacrilegious. And yet, it had doubtlessly saved his life and got him out of that hell alive.

He decided not to wash it off. He needed all the help he could get.

First, he had Victor to thank for distracting the demon guards and for Will evading detection. He shuddered at the thought of those monstrous, ugly motherfuckers. Their huge, muscular bulk and reptilian, scaly gray skin; their bulging dead eyes and cruel mouths. Worse, their huge, powerful hands with their poisonous-looking red talons that he imagined could rip off his arms very easily. Then his head.

He shook his head in the mirror, grateful that it was still in place at all.

Will couldn't believe how easily he had managed to escape out of the Darkness, following Victor's telepathic instructions. Nor how, amazingly, he had appeared to go unnoticed by all the demons and other beings he had passed by, as if he had acquired the power of invisibility. It was beyond incredible. And that's why he was doubting his judgment.

Without even thinking, when he reached the portal, he had managed to pass easily through it, emerging in the basement of the Madison House, from which he had simply unlocked the doors, run out of the yard, outside the fenced-off area of the construction site and away, to the main street. Within minutes, he had been able to catch a cab to his car, then driving here to this motel a few miles outside Melas. Thankful for relative safety, after living on adrenalin for the past few days, he had gradually sunk into a deep, much-needed sleep. He seemed to have slept through a whole day.

On reflection, it had been almost too easy. Why had Victor Rothenstein, of all people – vampire, mass murderer and arch-enemy of all that was holy – helped him?

But Victor's earnest face came back into his mind. His desperate expression, and his eyes wide with genuine fear! This ancient, dangerous vampire was terrified of what Jackie intended to do.

Terrified of the inadvertent unleashing of The Red Beast of Hell.

And now, it was down to Will to help Victor Rothenstein to prevent the Apocalypse.

***

White-knuckled as he held onto the leather steering wheel, Mike Moran drove into Melas, his face set grimly in a frown. Whatever the hell was happening on his construction site, he wanted it stopped. Now.

As Donovan Smith's business partner in the construction company, he had a real vested interest in people moving to Melas. And for that to happen, the housing and facilities needed to be constructed on time. And therefore, Mike was furious that some random psycho-killer was terrorising people, scaring people out of the area, and putting their contract deadline in jeopardy. Not to mention killing some workers.

As if it wasn't bad enough, Don had reported that some wimpy, cowardly workers were refusing to work onsite at all. And getting security working overnight was damn near impossible. The client, Jackie Nixon, had insisted on harsh penalties being written into the contract. She had been desperate for the town to be rebuilt as fast as possible – starting with her own house. Therefore, she had imposed a clause demanding crippling compensation if the deadline slipped and the construction wasn't completed on time. Despite Don's warnings about the severity of the penalties, Mike had agreed to this. After all, Jackie had been very even-handed in her offers. If they completed the old Madison house ahead of time and to a high standard, so that Jackie could move in as soon as possible, she had promised a bonus of eighty thousand dollars for every day ahead of schedule that the house was completed. Mike's eyes had gleamed with greed at the thought of this, and he had placed tremendous pressure on Don to flog his team hard to win as big a prize as soon as possible. Under duress, and with Don's eagerness to please Jackie, they had met that early completion date easily, achieving an additional eight hundred and eighty thousand dollars in pure profit. On one home alone! Although not nearly so generous for other buildings, the incentives she had offered for early completion of every other construction were compelling, too. Mike had seen millions of dollars of clear profit – in advance of the end of the contract – dancing before his eyes. But the price they had to pay for delays were financially debilitating – and horrifyingly, they were now on a course to default on the agreement to deliver on time. If this problem wasn't resolved soon, their whole business could come crashing around their ears.

And that's why they needed to sort this out – and fast.

Sure, Mike had warned Don to keep the client sweet. It was Jackie Nixon, after all, the most powerful woman in the area. And if that meant sleeping with her, then so be it. Jackie had clearly taken a shine to Donovan Smith, and Mike wanted to cash in on that. It could mean more contracts in future. Good connections. Millions more. Finance was Mike's part in the company. Don was the practical one. The overseer. The doer. And if that meant 'doing' Jackie Nixon – then, great! Mike Moran certainly wasn't averse to pimping out his partner if it meant more money for him, in the long run.

He pulled up outside the nearest bar to the construction site, just outside Melas, and looked around uneasily.

What kind of place is this? he wondered. *Will my car be OK parked here?*

It was fine for Don Smith, with his modest sport utility vehicle and his humble ways. But Mike's Jaguar F-Type Series looked to be more expensive than this whole damn bar. And its parking lot. And all the cars parked in it.

Reluctantly, he pressed the car-lock on his key fob, and went inside.

With any luck, this will take an hour, and I can get back in the car and drive.

He saw Don Smith at a table and raised one arm in greeting, before going to the bar counter after observing that Don was nursing a full glass himself. He noticed also that Don looked white and anxious.

So you should be. So many delays already. Get your finger out, thought Mike, ordering a beer. He sucked the first inch of beer off the top of the glassful and carried it over at arm's length, wary of the beer dribbling over his expensive hand-made suit.

"How's things?" he said breezily, sitting down opposite Don.

"Not good. Not good at all," Don said tightly. "Alison is still missing, and the police are no help."

Alison. Like Don's perfectly adequate, modest vehicle, Alison was Don's perfectly functional, modest wife. Although, admittedly, she seemed to have disappeared.

"Probably got wind of you and Jackie," Mike suggested, taking another slurp of beer. "Run off somewhere."

Don's eyes flashed. "I have been more than discreet!"

"Yeah, but no woman likes to be replaced…"

"I'd never replace her! I love Al!" Don yelled. "I never shoulda listened to you and got into this."

"Hey! Hey!" Mike said, raising one supplicatory palm. "It was just a suggestion. 'Keep Jackie sweet,' can be interpreted in many ways… Nobody forced you. And I thought you enjoyed bang-… '*being with*' - Jackie?" He mimed quotation marks in the air to emphasise his euphemism.

"I love my wife," Don said angrily. "And she's vanished…"

"She'll just be lying low, cooling off. You'll hear from her soon. Via her lawyer, probably."

"Fuck!" Don slammed his fist on the table-top, his eyes blazing with anger. "There are women missing – people dead! Anything could have happened to her!"

"Yeah. Hey, I'm sorry, man," Mike backtracked, realizing that Don was closer to the edge than he had imagined. "But… have faith."

"Faith in who? What? The police? God?"

"In Alison." Mike shrugged. "She's an intelligent woman. I'm sure she'll be okay."

"Yeah…" On reflection, Don conceded that Alison was a capable woman, worthy of his trust. He wiped his hand across his tired face. "It's just… All this… I feel so helpless."

"Yeah. And I want to help, Don. That's why we're meeting."

Don glanced up at Mike's earnest face, searching his concerned eyes. But he knew Mike well, and knew how he worked.

After a moment, Don shook his head and said wryly, "Mike - you know you're no good at the emotional stuff. Stick to what you're best at."

"I won't ask you what that is," Mike grinned. "Any more than I'll guess what Jackie thinks *you're* best at."

Don frowned pointedly at him, then threw back a mouthful of beer. He wiped his mouth. "I really don't know how come we're still friends."

"Because I have a great business mind," Don winked. "And make us plenty of money. Stick with me kid, and you'll be wearing diamonds."

Don couldn't conceal a smile, in spite of himself. "So let's talk about business. That's why we're here."

Mike nodded gratefully. Now he was on firmer ground. "So – tell me what contingencies we can get in place to deal with all this shit. How are we going to meet the deadlines?"

Don pulled himself around and sublimated his emotions into a practical solution, which would take them forward to fulfil the contract without incurring penalties. It would involve bringing in more agency staff, employing teams of armed security guards, floodlighting all relevant areas and working around the clock for a few weeks to catch up on the schedule. Maybe to even get ahead – and win some more bonuses. It would involve some additional investment, but that was nothing in comparison with the punitive penalties for failure.

Satisfied with their plans, Mike glanced at his expensive wristwatch. An hour had gone by, and he liked to keep business meetings tight.

"Looks like the rest of these guys are in for the night," he nodded towards the other clientele in the bar. "But I gotta go." He stood up.

Don also scraped his chair back with a screech. "Well, I'm in no mood for drinking. I'm off home, too."

In the dark parking lot, Don walked with Mike towards his luxury car, stopping halfway between his own SUV and Mike's sportscar. In the moonlight, while muttering final pieces of advice and instructions to Don, Mike casually examined the gleaming paintwork for signs of key scratching or damage. There was so much envy in the world. It was criminal. He ran his hand down the sleek side of the car, satisfied by its smooth perfection.

"Yeah, so like I said, get onto Jameson's and agree that we spend no…" A thunderous sound in the air interrupted Mike's speech. "What the…?"

They both looked up in wonder, but saw only blackness. A mighty wind, like the disturbance of air caused by a helicopter landing, swept their hair and clothes and stung their eyes. A huge dark shadow loomed above their frozen forms, and then massive leathery wings plunged down and wrapped around Mike where he stood, screaming.

Donovan Smith was a brave man who had seen many terrible things, but he was completely paralyzed with fear, unable to even blink or swallow.

At the hideous screeches of the dying man, several customers from the bar came running out of the front door, but stopped in horror.

The massive bat-like creatures – two of them, at least, by Don's reckoning – swooped off, and Mike's lifeless body crashed to the ground.

Appalled, no one could move for two seconds. Then Don launched himself forward and dropped to his knees next to Mike's inert form. In the light from the open bar door, he could see that Mike's throat had been ripped out, dark blood still pumping out into a pool beneath his head and the whites of his wild, open eyes still gleamed in an expression of terror.

***

After the chaos of screaming and shouting, the departure of the ambulance and the lengthy police interview, Don drove home, still shaking with fear. Apart from the direct trauma of witnessing his friend and business partner being mortally savaged by unearthly creatures, other thoughts troubled him that were much more than survivor guilt.

How come they attacked Mike and not me?

It wasn't an instinctive, emotional reaction that caused him concern – there was too much pain for that, and he blocked it with logic. It was a factual, analytical pondering that obsessed him.

There were two of them! Wouldn't two huge creatures – when faced with two vulnerable humans – prey on one each?

It surely wasn't that it necessitated two of them to bring down a human. They were massive creatures in size. If anything, they hindered one another in their feeding frenzy – their vast leathery wings flapping and clashing together, and their black foxy heads butting against one another to reach Mike's throat in the couple of seconds the attack had lasted. They had practically decapitated him. Why would two of them set upon one victim, when another was readily available to them?

In fact, if anyone was a prime target – wasn't it himself – Donovan Smith – standing openly in the middle of the car park, surrounded by empty space, rather than Mike, leaning against his car, protected on one side by it? But strangely, the monsters had targeted Mike – had only killed Mike, and left Don completely alone.

It didn't make sense!

And those creatures themselves. Don slammed the car door and unlocked his house, still deep in thought. All he could tell the police was, "Vampire bats. Huge, superhuman vampire bats."

The police had breathalyzed Don and had checked with the bartender to determine how much he had drunk. One beer had not induced the hallucinations he was reporting. But by the time they had rushed out, alerted by Mike's screams, the other people at the bar had seen nothing – reporting only that the sky was blacker than usual – the moon apparently blotted out by cloud – or something. One said he thought he saw a big, dark shadow move across the sky, but he couldn't be sure. The police had taken his statement, but had looked askance when he had described what he'd seen. After all, it was completely unbelievable.

Don, however, for the first time in his life, began to believe in supernatural forces. There was no logical, reasonable way to account for what he had seen. Yes, he still found it difficult to believe, and he didn't blame the police for doubting him. Now they had proof that he wasn't drunk, their only recourse was to consider him crazy. Having no evidence that Don had murdered his partner – no blood on him, no weapon in evidence – the officer's explanation was 'bear attack'. Don's grief over his missing wife must have made him delirious. He had imagined that the bear was a vampire bat!

Don knew better. He couldn't help feeling that all these strange deaths and disappearances – and Alison's vanishing without a word – were connected. And the only link he had with Alison's possible whereabouts were the books she had been reading recently, and the notes she had been taking. He had told the police she was investigating something, but they weren't interested in those details at this stage.

"Give her time," the investigating officer had said. "She'll turn up. It sounds as if she's found out about your affair and gone to cool off."

"With no clothes and no luggage?" Don asked, in bewilderment.

"You'd be surprised. Some people storm out with nothing. You know she took her purse and bank cards."

He knew she had taken a backpack, too, which was strange in itself. Alison wasn't a backpacking type at all. But he couldn't tell what else.

But it had been a number of days now, and their bank account had remained untouched. Don checked several times a day, hoping to see a withdrawal or a sale that he hadn't made. To no avail.

Also, there was something niggling him that he hadn't told the police, for fear that it would just add to their argument that she had lost it – she left him, in an emotional state. Alison had become oddly absorbed – and obsessed with the supernatural. She had always had a professional interest, of course. After all, she was Senior Lecturer in Occult Studies at West Virginia University, currently on a sabbatical to write her book: *Superstition in the Modern Age*. But her interest in the paranormal had always been as a sceptic – a debunker of crazy talk. But most recently, she had been rambling about seeing ghosts herself and warning him not to rebuild the old Madison House – Jackie's new home. But maybe the two weren't connected at all. Don had a strange inkling that Alison might know more about his affair than he thought. Maybe, even subconsciously, she had been jealous, or trying to keep him away from Jackie?

But Alison was a studious, rational person. Her real sense of alarm and genuine fear about him rebuilding the old mansion had been way beyond anything he'd seen in her before, and he had a suspicion that it was linked to her research into materials for her new book. And that somehow, this all linked to the recent strange deaths, disappearances, and the horrific supernatural experience he'd had that night.

Therefore, despite his exhaustion and trauma, as dawn broke and dim light filtered into his home, Don headed straight for Alison's study, which was a tumble of books and papers. *Typical mad professor!* he used to joke with her. He glanced around, noting the usual piles of books on the floor, the open book on the desk, the closed notebook with a pen lying on top of it, and the scattered loose-leaf papers – numerous prints of online research for the academic book she was writing; a draft of the manuscript to date, and typed and handwritten notes that littered Alison's desk.

Where to begin?

He sat down in Alison's office chair, feeling strangely intrusive, and lifted the book that was open in front of him, flipping it over to read the title on the spine. The worn gilt lettering read: *BAPHOMET REALIZED* and the name: *W. PINKMAN.* He flipped back to the page where the book had been left open, and skim-read it. Lots of words and sentences that seemed dully scholarly and occasionally slightly manic in tone, but nothing that meant anything to him. He flicked through the earlier pages, presuming that those were ones that Alison must have read recently. He stopped dead as his eye caught an illustration on one page – a drawing of a winged, bat-like creature with a goat's head! It was evidently a copy of an ancient engraved plate. But beneath the old print, there were Latin words that Don could not understand. Flicking through, he saw other similar illustrations. It looked Satanic – a bit like the old images of the Devil he'd seen in old horror movies – a horned head, but a human body. From the passages Don read of the text, although written in a densely academic tone, it seemed to be something about the history, worship and summoning of this demonic entity. But despite the huge black wings, this was not the creature that had attacked Mike. He was sure of that. Those monsters were huge, black bats. Slightly taller than Mike with ridiculously large wingspans. But still – this seemed like too much of a coincidence…

Appalled, Don stared blankly at the handwritten notes Alison had made, and began shuffling through Alison's ancient occult papers for further clues.

CHAPTER 5

Jackie and Kate had made it back to the Madison House, fleeing the carpark outside the bar first on wings, and then, afraid of being seen flying into the grounds of Jackie's house, they had dropped into the sparse woodland just outside the new construction site in Melas, and transformed back into their female human forms. They had usually managed the whole hunting expedition as bats on previous occasions, but having been seen by Donovan Smith – and possibly by the people who rushed to the door of the bar – they knew they could not fly directly home, for fear that others might track their flight and put two and two together.

They were back in their normal human, American clothing, rather than their vampirically Gothic evening gowns, and hastily set off from the center of the woods, heading for home.

"We should have brought the car and parked it here," grumbled Kate, trying to maneuver the rocky ground in her high heels.

"Now you tell me," Jackie snorted. "And yet, you were keen enough to fly directly from the Vampire Castle – such was your greed."

Kate lunged sideways, grabbing onto her mother's sleeve, as her ankle turned. "Sorry," she muttered, as Jackie snatched her arm away.

"You're only irritated because that guy saw us," Kate said. In her bat-form, she had received the psychic instruction from her mother to attack only the man near the car. "Although why we couldn't go for him, too, I don't know. We should remove all witnesses. I can't imagine why you stopped me."

"Because I know him," Jackie said tightly.

Kate frowned. "All the more reason to eliminate him, then."

"I have my reasons."

They made the rest of the short walk through the spindly trees in brooding silence.

On the floodlit road, they approached the security gate in the fence around the Melas construction site, through which they needed to enter to get to Jackie's house, and saw the two guards leap to attention in surprise. One shone his torch directly into Jackie's face, its harsh beam leaching what little color there was out of her face.

"Ladies!" the one with the torch said, lowering the yellow light when he realized who they were; his eyes wide in shock as he walked towards them. "Don't you know it's dangerous to wander around after dark?"

"Pshaw!" Jackie said dismissively, marching through the gate. "I own this whole place."

"Still, Ma'am… for your safety…"

Jackie marched swiftly on, on past the guards, Kate hobbling beside her on her ridiculous heels.

Kate muttered in a low voice to her mother, "Where do we say we've been?"

"I am accountable to no one, Kate." Jackie spat. "Least of all, to humans."

They quickly walked on along the main road into Melas, and turned into Racoon Run Road, which led to the old Madison house – their new home.

Jackie kept a watchful eye on the dark sky above them, and on the horizon ahead, where the sun would rise. At the least sign of dawn and breaking daylight, they would be in terrible danger. A vampire could never survive the touch of sunlight – they would dissolve into ashes if a single sunbeam broke forth while they were at large in the world. Although there were ways and means to pass as a human, as Jackie and Kate were discovering. Indeed, remembering her own father – Walter Pinkman's – devoted service to Victor Rothenstein, Jackie was altogether aware of the guiles vampires used to keep their secrets whilst pretending to be ordinary human beings.

Jackie and Kate were managing their dual life quite well, so far. They spent time in the Darkness, in the realms that Jackie believed herself to rule over, as Empress of the Darkness – flying through to the Vampire Castle to pump Victor for information and progress Jackie's preparations for raising her vampire army. In the human world, Jackie had another empire to manage – overseeing her businesses and the reconstruction of the town of Melas by day – and either attending board meetings after dark, or hunting human prey by night for the fresh blood she craved. Her daughter, Kate, was almost constantly by her side.

Claiming a strange sun allergy, they now never left the Madison House during daylight hours, relying on Jackie's staff and business partners to visit the house for important meetings and to attend to the day-to-day operational business on her behalf.

A week or so before, everything was normal – then the house was initially draped with blackout curtains – until Jackie had suddenly requested the replacement of all the windows in the house with tinted glass that cut out all ultraviolet rays.

"You never mentioned this before," Don had scowled, after being called in personally as chief construction manager, to discuss Jackie's new requests. "We could have done that at the outset, had we known, and saved you all the expense – and upheaval."

"Fuck the expense," Jackie shrugged casually, but gave him a steady, assured look that defied him to challenge her. "Things change. My condition is much worse than it's ever been. So you can make the changes now."

"Fair enough," Don had conceded. But he still wondered why Jackie had been able to sun herself on her husband's yacht only a few months ago, before he died, and how many vacations she had been on, to hot countries… and why this sun allergy had suddenly appeared – with a real vengeance. Weren't people usually born with these life-threatening conditions? As far as he was aware, they didn't happen overnight. But who was he to argue? It was her money. Her specifications. She was the boss. Dammit, because of Mike's persuasion and insistence, she was Don's mistress in all senses of the word.

***

Having read Alison's notes, Don was none the wiser. Much of it was clearly drafts of her central ideas for her book, or full-scale sections of her manuscript on superstition. She had, however, left the last written page of her notebook that said:

Walter Pinkman - necromancy.
Madison House - Investigate.

It was all Don had to go on. He went to see Jackie.

As had become the usual custom over the last week or so, a servant opened the front door and showed him into the dusky filtered light of the living room. Jackie clearly was taking no risks of any sunlight hitting her at all.

"Why, Don!" she squealed, playing up the role of doting female. "To what do I owe this *pleasure*?"

She sprang up and draped her arms around his neck, kissing him full on the lips. Don stood there uneasily, his closed lips non-compliant. These days, for some reason, Don trusted her even less than usual. He was deeply troubled.

Kissing his stiff, unmoving mouth, Jackie recoiled in concern. She stared at him. "What's the matter? Don't you luuur-rve me anymore?" she teased.

I never loved you. I love Alison, Don thought.

"I love Alison," he said.

"Of course you do," Jackie smiled indulgently. "Your lovely plain, mousy, bookish wife. I know you do, Don. Of course you do. She is lovely! No threat, no challenge." She waved her highly polished fingernails dismissively. "No big deal."

She pressed her cool hand onto his chest, stroking it firmly across his shirt until one finger crept between the buttons and touched his skin. Her tongue delicately, slowly, licked her lips.

Don swallowed, feeling his cock harden in spite of himself. But despite the blood rushing from his head, he still had sufficient sense to say what he'd come here for.

"Alison is gone. Do you have any idea where? What's happened to her?"

Jackie's eyebrows shot up as far as they could in her botoxed forehead. "Why, no! I have no idea where she is. I haven't seen her for months. We don't exactly mix in the same circles, Don."

He stared into her eyes, trying to make out whether or not she was telling the truth. He was so beaten down, he had no faith in his own perceptions any more.

"You're my only hope," he said sadly.

She frowned.

"Besides, why would I want to get rid of her?" Jackie asked, genuinely. "You're great in bed, Don, but that's it." She traced her hand right down from his chest to his crotch, cupping him in her hand and squeezing his hardness. "Speaking of which… why don't we go and… give you some release?"

Don exhaled a great, heaving breath. The last thing in the world he wanted to do was make love with Jackie, and yet his penis thought otherwise.

"You're so tense, Don." Still holding his balls firmly through his jeans, Jackie stood on tiptoe and breathed moistly into his ear, "I can give you some loving comfort, Don. Or you can ride me hard – vent some of that repressed anger. The choice is yours."

His cock twitched, but Don resisted. "I'm sorry, Jackie. It's tempting and you're an irresistible woman, but… I'm so…" Don's lip quivered with emotion.

Jackie gave his crotch an extra squeeze, but he took her wrist and gently prised her hand off.

"I'm just too upset. I don't… It's Alison… I'm worried and I just can't, Jackie. I'm sorry."

"Poor baby," Jackie pouted, but not unkindly. She lifted her hand to his cheek and softly wiped away the single tear he had shed.

"I don't know what to do, Jackie…" He bent his head down, covered his eyes with one hand and wept.

"Oh, Don." Jackie slipped her hand around the back of his neck, and pressed her mouth to his throat in a soft kiss. She felt the pulsation of blood under his skin, and breathed hard. Her eyes gleamed widely and her lip curled, exposing her fangs. Poised only a hair's breadth from his carotid artery, with immense self-control, she pulled away, panting hard.

"Tomorrow," she breathed. "Come again tomorrow. I want you. If you will help me… to relax… I will help you."

He gazed into her eyes. She was a powerful woman, in more ways than one. Maybe she could help. She had money and influence. She might pay for some private investigators who might actually take his concerns seriously. Or – if she was involved in Alison's disappearance at all – or if there was something to do with the house that had made Alison disappear – maybe he would find out more. Discover why Alison was obsessed with the Madison House and had begged him not to rebuild it. One way or another, as long as he kept his wits about him, he could use Jackie to find Alison. All he had to do was please Jackie, and she would help him. It was no worse than sleeping with her to protect his business, as he had been doing all these months. Once a prostitute... But this time, he wanted to be the one in control. The one calling the shots. All he had to do was keep his head, in the face of her seductiveness.

"Let's meet tomorrow afternoon," she said, opening her mouth and pressing it against his.

Gratefully, he returned her kiss, deeply.

CHAPTER 6

The next day, Donovan Smith was ostensibly at work in the construction site office, revisiting the blueprints of the old Madison House. He stood, head bent over the desk, leaning his palms on the pale gray-blue diagrams. There were no surprises there. He hardly knew why he was checking these sheets again. The house was finished, and he didn't need the drawings to remind him of its composition. He knew these drawings like the back of his hand, plus all of the odd specifications Jackie had given him since they had commenced the reconstruction. Her demands that they incorporate human body ashes that made up the silt from the lake that had flooded the town, and stones from the old Pinkman house into the new building that was to be her home.

That was freaky enough, to be sure. *A tribute to the dead. A memorial to the past*, Jackie had said. He had been almost convinced, at the time.

But what the hell was it that had freaked out Alison so much about the house? Far more than he had been freaked out by Jackie's strange requests. Alison had been so desperately adamant that the Madison House should not be rebuilt – she had cried and implored Don not to do it. But he thought she was being irrational and unreasonable. Egged on by Mike's request that they pander to their rich client's every whim, Don had carried out all of Jackie's wishes. The house was completed – Jackie had moved in – and Alison had gone missing.

She had left her notes and research – and her beloved manuscript – scattered across her desk, like a scene of hurried abandonment from the Marie Celeste. What had Alison read in her research findings, or heard? What did she know, that had made her grab a backpack in the middle of the night, and go off somewhere, never to be seen again? It was deeply troubling.

"Where is she?" Don said aloud.

"Dead," came a distant voice.

Don spun round, on guard, his eyes bulging, searching for the owner of the voice. There was no one there. Frowning, he shook his head like someone whose hearing has been affected by diving into deep water. His ears deceived him.

Preoccupied, he turned back around and stared at the drawings again.

"She's dead."

Don jumped a foot in the air, rattling his chair so that it almost overturned. A young woman, clear as day, but slightly transparent and ethereal, was standing at his elbow.

"F… wh - who?" Don stuttered, his heart pounding out of his chest.

"Lucy. Lucy Westerna," said Lucy Westerna's ghost.

She was exactly as Alison had described her, when she had rambled incoherently – as far as Don was concerned – about seeing a ghost by the name of Lucy

Westerna. But Don had disbelieved his wife – considered her hysterical or overworked. Suspected her of beginning the first stages of a mental breakdown. And now, was he crazy, himself? Driven mad by grief?

His mouth dry and open in amazement, he could only gawp at the apparition before him.

"Alison is dead," the ghost repeated, in a measured tone.

"Wha…?" Don's dry throat expelled a croaking sound. "How?"

"Killed by Kate in the Darkness."

"Kate?" Don was astounded. Jackie's daughter had only recently come on the scene – in fact, Jackie had never even mentioned having a daughter until she turned up a few days ago. Don scoured his memory. In fact, Kate had arrived in Melas *after* Alison disappeared. She wasn't even around – wouldn't even know Alison. This made no sense at all. It couldn't be true.

"You're…" Don commenced, in bewilderment. "The ghost that Alison talked about… the… that warned Alison… That was you?"

The spirit of Lucy Westerna spoke calmly, reassuringly, as if aware that Don was questioning his own sanity. "Yes, what Alison told you was true. Beware of the Madison House," she warned. "Jackie Nixon requested that you construct the house in such a way as to channel the profound energies of the past, and of the underworld."

She swept an elegant, translucent arm above the blueprints, long wispy fingers indicating the basement levels of the drawing of the building. "You built into the foundations some powerful elements of ancient magical potency, hitherto lost in history and only known by academic repute. The burnt remains, ashes and bones of the dead of Melas, who suffered in the asylum fire, were utilized. These local areas were flooded and the human remains became buried in the base of the lake, ash, bone and cindered flesh combining with the lakebed mud to create the clay and sand you used in the bricks and concrete for the basement of the renovation."

Don frowned, deep in thought. *Am I hallucinating?*

And yet, the ghost spoke reasonably. "The specific polished stones and pebbles that Jackie Nixon demanded that you embed into the design as features are actually the essence of human souls – entrapped in a physical form called 'soul stones' – solidified by the ritual magic practised by Walter Pinkman, Jackie Nixon's father."

"Walter Pinkman?" Don gasped. The '*W. Pinkman*' whose book lay open on Alison's desk? The book about Baphomet, the goat-faced demonic creature with huge bat-wings! Don had only been flicking through the odd textbook in the early hours of the day before. Alison – Walter Pinkman – Jackie Nixon's father? The connections were too real to be ignored. This was all too much of a coincidence to be untrue.

"Indeed," the ghost continued. "The purpose of utilizing the lake sediment and soul stones was to set the basis for some powerful, evil spells. The fateful setting – Melas, the site of the Madison House – and the intensity of focussed energy from the spirits of the dead enabled Jackie Nixon to activate the powerful portal to the Darkness beneath."

Don still didn't understand. When the spirit mentioned the Darkness, he had no concept of it as another world. He literally thought she meant the dark earth.

"Portal?" Don queried. "Like a door? Leading to where?"

"The Darkness," Lucy Westerna repeated.

Seeing Don's blank look, she elaborated. "The Darkness is a place of tortured souls; of evil souls – a Hell of sorts. But there is far worse to come, if Jackie Nixon has her way."

Don stood in wonder, waiting for an explanation, and trying to assimilate the knowledge that had already been revealed to him. This was all too much to take in.

"The house is growing ever stronger, and ever more evil," Lucy warned Don. "Jackie Nixon herself has no idea how powerful the Madison House is now. Or can become . . . She knows not what she does."

Don swallowed hard. If he wasn't dreaming… if he wasn't simply sleep-deprived and delusional… could this really be true? And if what this ghost was saying was, in fact, true… He slapped his forehead with his palm.

"Alison is dead?" he cried.

"I'm sorry. Yes," Lucy said softly.

"She's dead, you say?" he turned his desperate, sorrowful eyes towards the ghost's shadowed, hollow ones. Realization steadily crossed his face and entered his consciousness. All his niggling fears were confirmed. "But… but…" His face screwed up in disbelief, the edge of grief fraying. "Why? How?"

"She got too close to the truth," Lucy said sadly. "Curiosity killed the cat, but she was no merely curious, scholarly investigator. Her interest was not just theoretical. She took action. She wanted to stop the progress of evil, so ventured to the Madison House. There, the veil between the worlds is thin, and she became... absorbed. She found her way into the Darkness, and battled with Kate, Jackie's daughter. She lost."

Don stared at her. His mind was making complicated calculations, weighing facts against unknowns; dividing possibilities by probability. Believing the words of a phantom? It was all he had to go on. Ironically, it was the closest thing to an explanation that made sense he had received.

"She died valiantly," added Lucy.

Whereas, I am a coward, Don thought bitterly. *I did as Mike told me. I allowed myself to be used. I didn't listen to Alison. I didn't stand up to Jackie. It's my fault Alison is dead.*

Don gulped. Effectively, he himself had sacrificed his own wife. If only he had listened to Alison instead of dismissing her!

"If I hadn't built the house... If I hadn't done exactly as Jackie asked... then... Alison would still be alive?"

"Indeed," Lucy confirmed. "But worse than that..."

There is nothing worse! Don's thoughts raged. *Alison is dead! I could have prevented it! Instead, I signed her death warrant!*

"A single individual's death is as nothing, compared with the wholesale, large-scale apocalypse that Jackie

Nixon plans. What she has in mind with unleash terror on the world – destroying millions of souls."

Don frowned. "That's impossible, surely? That would be completely inhuman."

"Correct," nodded Lucy. "Jackie Nixon is completely inhuman. She is a vampire."

Don spluttered, almost choking in disbelief. "Ridiculous!"

Lucy stared at him steadily, in silence. Don met the unseeing gaze of her hooded eyes; but still she said nothing, allowing the information to sink in. *Vampires don't exist,* he told himself.

Vampires. Vampire bats. That was what he had told the police. That was how he had described the huge creatures that had attacked and killed Mike. Their leathery wings and fox-like heads looked just like bats' distinctive features. They had ripped out Mike's throat – and sucked his blood, like vampires. Unaccountably, they had left Don alone and allowed him to live.

Why? he wondered. *Because Jackie likes me? Because she wants me? Because I am useful to her – even just for sex?*

Again, as if she had access to Don's thoughts, Lucy finally told Donovan, "It's all true. Jackie Nixon simply used you as a pawn in her game – to achieve her own selfish ends."

Then Lucy Westerna's ghost disappeared as suddenly as she had arrived. Leaving Donovan Smith dumbfounded.

***

That very afternoon found Don on the doorstep of the Madison House, as previously arranged with Jackie Nixon the day before. Grim determination etched his concerned face. This particular time had been scheduled to be their afternoon of lovemaking, but there was nothing further from his mind than this. Besides, the deal had been that if he 'helped' Jackie, she would help him – yet, if what Lucy Westerna's ghost had said was true, it seemed that Alison was beyond help.

Don still needed answers. He still wasn't sure he could believe a phantom voice – especially when he didn't even believe in ghosts, up until this morning. His rational mind had kicked in again, and he wasn't certain what to think of his recent experience. Imagination? Mental illness? Or reality? He'd been under tremendous pressure recently, and had missed a lot of sleep, which he knew could make people delusional – and this was the main reason he doubted himself. Perhaps he really was losing his mind. He needed to confront Jackie for himself, and see if he could identify the truth.

Before he rang the doorbell of Jackie Nixon's house – the old Madison property, rebuilt – he gazed at the basement level of the house, where the bulk of the strange requests had centered upon. The stern slits of the low basement windows seemed to scrutinize him, like malevolent eyes. Was that just his imagination, too?

He took a deep breath, remembering Lucy Westerna's words. *The house is evil.*

He wondered if he should feel something – some brooding atmosphere; some demonic presence. He felt nothing but trepidation – a purely human emotion that was understandable, given that he was planning a very direct conversation with a formidable woman who wielded a great deal of political and financial power. And sexual power. Over him.

He pressed his finger on the doorbell, almost in a trance.

Within seconds, Jackie's PA answered the door and let him through to the dimly-lit living room. The heavily tinted windows were extremely effective in cutting out not only the UV light, but much of the light at all. It looked to be permanently twilight throughout the house, regardless of the time of day or weather. Sunlight never penetrated beyond the threshold. And Jackie never crossed the threshold at all these days, until darkness had fallen. Such was the severity of her skin allergies. So she said.

Jackie Nixon lay lounging on the leather couch, propped up by scatter cushions. When the PA opened the door, and Don strode in, the door closing after him leaving them alone, Jackie sat up, beaming.

Despite her Gothic and vampiric appearance in the Darkness, with her purple or black hair in that realm, Jackie's figure, hairdressing and fashion sense in the human world were much as they had been when she was alive. Except, aside from her pallor, she was more vibrant. Her terminal cancer was gone, and the progress of her ageing had been arrested.

She tossed back her blonde hair flirtatiously, and rose from the couch, stalking across the room to greet Don, her limbs lithe and panther-like.

She pressed herself against Don's unyielding body. Like a well-choreographed dance movement in a seductive rumba, she slowly extended one arm and hooked her wrist around the back of Don's neck. Her long fingers wrapped themselves around his neck, the soft pads of her fingertips pressing gently on the side of his throat. She could feel his pulse, as the blood rushed through his arteries, and her pelvic floor gave an involuntary squeeze of sexual desire. She lifted one leg and snaked it around his side, her inner thighs hot against his leg as she straddled it.

"So good to see you, Don," she said, her voice husky with lust.

"I want the truth," Don said, his face impenetrable and his tone impassive.

Jackie froze, uncertainly. "It *is* good to see you. And that's the truth."

Don peeled Jackie's hand from his neck and stepped back, leaving her unstably rocking on her heels.

"Is it true that Alison is dead?" he barked. "And that your daughter killed her?"

Jackie laughed in disbelief. "Don... isn't that ridiculous?" Her eyes searched his, but she could see that he was deadly serious. His mouth was set in a determined grimace; his stare appraising her coolly.

Something about his sternness and his resistance to her charms was a turn-on to Jackie. Most people danced to her tune. She liked this masterful Donovan Smith. She gazed up at him in wonder.

"Tell me, Jackie," he commanded. "I want to hear it from your own mouth."

She stared him out, but he held her gaze until she was the one who blinked and turned away.

"Very well." Jackie cleared her throat. "True. Alison is dead. But it was an accident. She invaded my home,

103

and Kate merely reacted, as she would to any burglar who might be dangerous."

"And you didn't contact the police?" Don scowled at her. His doubt remained.

Jackie shrugged. "It's complicated."

"It's complicated?" scoffed Don. "*It's complicated?*"

Jackie stared into his eyes, trying to assess how much he knew for sure. Nothing, for sure – she could tell. But he did appear to know something.

"Is it as complicated as being a *vampire*?" Don said, his voice hard.

Jackie's mind reeled. But her eyes flickered in recognition, and even Don could not mistake the fact that he had hit upon a truth – no matter how unbelievable the fact might be.

"Where did you get your information?" she asked, calmly.

"I have my sources."

"Supernatural sources?" she asked, her tone very deliberate.

Don's silence spoke volumes. Jackie's mind raced, identifying possibilities. Who could have told him these things? *Victor Rothenstein*? But he had been under constant watch. *Kate?* Surely she would not betray them both! Besides, as Alison's killer, she was hardly likely to confess to Don, of all people.

Don spoke, steadily. "So. You are a vampire. And you're the ones I saw kill Mike."

Jackie stared into his eyes. Decided that there was no sense in lying. "Correct."

"But you saved me."

"I have a soft spot for you, Don. Just like I hope you have a *hard* spot for me…"

He interrupted: "So everything is correct. Alison is dead. Kate killed her. Mike is dead. You killed him. You're both vampires. And this… this house… you tricked me into giving it some evil power?"

Jackie shrugged. "Hardly 'tricked'. You did it all willingly…"

Don almost laughed. He shook his head, chuckling sarcastically. "You are unbelievable."

"You better believe it." She stepped towards him and lay both her hands on his chest. Running her tongue over her lips slowly, she sneered, "Does it turn you on?"

Don took both her wrists roughly and flung her hands off him. Jackie gasped. Her thin wrist-bones burned with the sharp pain of his tight grasp.

"You bastard!" she cried, but there was still an element of sexual excitement in her voice.

Don looked her straight in the eyes and spat, "You'll pay for this."

"Oh! What are you going to do? Tell the police?" she mocked. "I *pay* the police! Who are they going to believe? A half-crazy builder whose wife has left him? Whose partner was killed before his eyes? Or a wealthy, reputable businesswoman whose head is screwed on – who is investing in the local town, creating opportunities – a pillar of the community?" Her eyes shone with victory. "Get out before I change my mind and kill you myself!"

Don's mouth twisted in hatred. After staring at her in silence for a couple of seconds, he turned on his heel to leave.

"If you even dare talk – you will lose the contract to rebuild the town. I will destroy you!"

Her voice ringing in his ears, Don left the room and hurried out of the house.

Jackie had confirmed everything, including Don's greatest fears. Everything Lucy Westerna's ghost had said was true.

"You weak-minded, pathetic loser," she had murmured. "You only have yourself to blame."

Her words stung him. *Truth hurts!* he thought. But she wasn't saying anything he hadn't told himself.

Don flung himself into the driver's seat and slammed his car door. He felt shattered by her revelations. He kicked the engine into life, and roared off home.

CHAPTER 7

William had flown out to Cleveland, Ohio, to Herman Thayer's old house, in search of the Grimoire Țepeș.

The property was early twentieth century. *Maybe Victorian.* Will was bad at estimating these things. But it was a medium-sized shingle-roofed two-story building on a fairly large plot. The grass in the front yard was knee-high and tangled, and the flower beds overgrown, dotted with weeds and long-unkempt. As Will approached the front door, walking along the tiled pathway, he saw that some of the wooden siding was loose, and the paintwork on the windows and doors faded and peeling. It looked unlived-in. Certainly unloved.

Will wasn't certain if anyone would answer the door, but he knocked on it anyway. For all he knew, since Herman Thayer had died, the house might have been sold, and the place emptied. There might even be a new family living there. It was possible that there might be no sign of the book he required. But it was the only lead he had, and he needed to follow it. Victor's urging had been imperative.

He had waited a minute on the porch after knocking, to no avail, so hammered at the brass door knocker again.

Will was just casting his eyes to the windows to see how easily they might be prised open, and considering walking around to the back, where he could break into the house unseen from the road, when the door suddenly opened, and a small, petite woman in her early thirties, wearing skinny jeans and a red plaid shirt stood on the threshold, a tea towel in her hands.

"Hello?" she said querulously, busily wiping her wet hands on the towel.

William observed that she had a pretty face, even without makeup, but her wary demeanour made her appear mousy and shy.

"Good evening." It was only five o'clock and still light, but 'good afternoon' didn't seem appropriate. "I'm William McConnellson III," Will said brightly, extending his hand to shake hers.

She rubbed her right hand down the leg of her jeans, laughing nervously, "Oh, I'm sorry. My hands are damp..." She shook his hand daintily, and he noticed how tiny her bones were, fragile as a bird's, in his strong grip. "I'm Natasha Thayer," she said, her brow wrinkling into a frown, wondering who he was and why he was here.

In his leather jacket, white T-shirt and crumpled jeans, he looked too casually dressed to be a Jehovah's Witness or a Mormon, or a door-to-door salesman. But why would a stranger knock on someone's door?

Will's heart had leapt when she said her name. *Thayer!* The house was in the same family! The book was safe – all being well!

"Um," he cleared his throat and gave her his most winning, self-effacing smile. He had already picked up that she was a little timid and nervous, so he didn't want to overwhelm her with a full-on charm offensive. He sought to match her energy, and build her trust first. He needed her help, so was careful to use a measured approach to win her over.

"Are you Herman Thayer's daughter?" he asked hopefully.

"His niece," she said, in surprise. "Why do you ask?"

"I was sent here by a friend of your uncle's," he said, shrugging slightly and holding out his hands in a gesture of helplessness that he knew appealed to women. It suggested that he was a harmless young man, who needed looking after. "I was told you might help!"

Natasha was entranced by his boyish good looks and his mild manner. His blue eyes were kindly and earnest, and she was completely charmed. She stood smiling at him, and he saw that her face had lit up with a radiance he hadn't anticipated. She looked beautiful!

Natasha suddenly shook herself out of the spell to exclaim, "Goodness! What am I doing, keeping you standing on the doorstep, then? I do apologize. Please come in!"

She ushered him through the echoing hallway and into a sparse kitchen. She chattered somewhat self-consciously, "So sorry to be so suspicious. I thought you might be from a religious cult or something!"

Will laughed genuinely. "Well, I used to be a priest, but I'm OK, now."

"*Really?*" she exclaimed, looking at him more closely. "You don't look the type!"

Will laughed, and she added quickly, "Oh, I'm sorry. I don't mean to offend, I mean – you don't look stuffy or serious and… well, you look so young!"

"I'm older than you think," he said, meaningfully, staring her deeply in the eyes. "Plenty old enough."

Natasha gulped, her mouth dry. This was a very attractive young man. And now knowing that he had once been a priest, she was both reassured and intrigued. She'd already had a good feeling about him as soon as she met him, and now, knowing that he had been a man of God, she felt even safer and more comfortable with him.

A priest… So young? Unbidden, salacious thoughts came into her mind. *Is he a virgin?*

Surely not, a good-looking guy like him. She blushed at the thoughts she was having, and brought her mind to the tasks at hand.

"Please – sit down." She gestured to a spindly kitchen chair tucked underneath a yellow Formica table.

She offered him some freshly made filter coffee that was kept warm on the hotplate. Will gratefully accepted, and, turning her back on him to pour the coffee, Natasha took the opportunity to recover her senses and pull herself together.

Meanwhile, with her back turned, Will took the opportunity to check out her tight ass cheeks, snugly moulded into her fitted jeans.

Passing him a mug, she grinned at him and asked, "So, how may I be of assistance?"

"I was told that your uncle has a copy of a rare book…" Will began, nursing the mug between his long fingers.

"Oh, he had many rare books," Natasha interrupted. "He was a well-known collector. I am just sifting through some of his things now, cataloging them in preparation for sale…"

William could hardly contain his delight. With any luck, she would know exactly where the Grimoire Țepeș was, could lay her hands on it straight away, and she might even sell it to him without any hesitation!"

He grinned. "That's brilliant."

I could be out of here within half an hour and on my way to the airport!

And yet… His eyes strayed to the shadowy cleft of her breasts, just visible in the V of the open neck of her plaid shirt.

He sipped the hot, bitter coffee, his eyes narrowing against the rising steam. Then he announced, "Because I'd love to have a copy – to buy, borrow, or even just to look at…"

He smiled bashfully, wanting to give the appearance of being unassuming, whilst covering all the bases.

"Certainly!" she returned his smile. "I'd love to help."

It was extraordinary, what that dazzling smile did for her otherwise unremarkable features.

She peered over into Will's mug, and bit her lip, gazing at him playfully. He watched the pressure of her teeth cause the blood to rush and redden her lips. If it wasn't just his imagination, those lips also seemed to have swollen, too. Pouting. He had an urge to kiss them. Thrust his tongue between them. Thrust... elsewhere, too...

"I could take you upstairs now!" she said brightly.

"What?" he was shocked out of his reverie. Had she read his mind?

"To my uncle's library!" she said, innocently unaware of his thinking, and she stood up. "Let's see if we can find what you're looking for." She paused, and he still wondered if she was flirting with him, before she added, "You can bring your coffee. As long as you don't take it near the books."

He nodded, amused, and followed her upstairs, his eyes trained on the muscles of her buttocks as she worked the stairs. His own jeans rubbed against his hardening erection as his thighs pumped the blood hard with each step he took after her.

Pull yourself together! he scolded himself. *This is serious business, for fucksake.*

For... fuck's... sake – Not only business – it would also be a pleasure... His mind wandered, imagining the two tiny, taut globes of her bottom cupped in his warm hands, as he lifted her up onto the head of his straining cock, then plunged her hips down, hot...

"What is it you want?" Natasha said at the top of the stairs.

"What?" he croaked, all reason lost.

"What book?"

She saw his red face, the sheen of sweat on his brow and his glazed, distracted look, and began to feel the slightest touch of unease. Maybe she was wrong to trust this stranger!

"Sorry," he murmured, trying to overcompensate for his sexual interest; trying to make excuses. "I just feel a little unwell. The traveling, I think. Jet lag, perhaps."

"Oh, my goodness!" she cried in concern, her hands flapping uselessly. "Do you need to sit down? Here – let me take that!" She removed the mug of coffee from his hand. "There are chairs in the library," she said, indicating a door off the landing. "Can I get you a drink of water or anything?"

Somewhere inside, a part of him was laughing heartily. *I've never seen a woman so attentive to a man's hard-on – without even realizing it!*

"No, I think I'll be OK," he said, trying to smile reassuringly, as she steered him into the library, one tiny hand gripped but barely able to hold his bulging bicep.

The first thing that struck him was the unmistakeable smell of old books – of dust, must, old leather and parchment. Oak shelving lined the room – half of it empty of books, the rest all in place. The floor was littered with cardboard boxes – some sealed, some empty – one half-full of books, with a stack of tissue paper, a pen and a checklist next to it, as if she had just been interrupted in the process of packing. Small piles of books surrounded them.

Natasha walked him to a leather armchair and sat him down. She bobbed down on her haunches next to him, on hand just above his knee. He was acutely aware of her touch.

"Are you OK?" Her hazel eyes showed concern.

113

"Yes. Yes." He felt such a fraud! "Much better for sitting down. And a hot drink. Thanks." He took the mug from her and slurped a mouthful of the cooling coffee.

"You're sure?" she asked, doubtfully. He nodded, and after pursing her lips in consideration, she decided that maybe the crisis was over.

She went on. "OK. If you're really sure… Well, I have a list of every item in the collection recorded here, and of the books I have already parcelled up." She walked across the room to a leather-topped desk and lifted up a ledger. "What was the book you wanted?"

"It's called *Grimoire Ţepeş*," Will said, beginning to spell it out: "G-R-I-M…"

"I don't believe it!" Natasha said, almost laughing in amazement.

"What?"

"I don't even have to look that one up!" she smiled. "I have been here, on and off, for months, clearing my uncle's house, sorting through his possessions, answering calls from buyers… And of all the books in all the collection – you have to mention that one!"

"What?" Will's stomach lurched. "Have you got the book?" His eyes were wild, and Natasha worried that his malaise had returned.

"No," she said. "I'm sorry. I haven't."

"You don't have a copy?" Will said in surprise. "But your uncle was…"

Will didn't know what to do. His hopes were dashed. He had to get his hands on that book!

"Yes, my uncle did have a copy of the Grimoire Ţepeş," she assured him. "But before his death, it was borrowed from him by a friend of his…"

"Who? Where is it? Who has it?" he interrupted, trying to modulate his tone, so as not to come across as desperate as he really was.

"Hold on," she flicked a few pages of the ledger, back and forth, before settling on one. "Here we are." She ran her finger down a handwritten list. "An... Alison Smith. She wanted it for some arcane research work. And she's yet to return it. It's the only book he owned that wasn't actually in his possession at the time of his death. I must chase that up, actually. You've just reminded me."

Will put his cards on the table. "I was going to ask you if I might buy it – or if you didn't want to let it go... to borrow it for a while?"

Natasha gave an apologetic shrug. "I'm sure that would have been fine, William, but unfortunately, until Ms Smith gives it back..." Her lips twisted in an expression of helplessness.

"Do you think we could discuss terms... prices, anyway?" Will persisted. "Theoretically? Just so the path is laid out ready, for when she... does bring it back?"

Natasha blew out an exhalation of air. *Those plump rosebud lips again!*

"Do you have some contact details for her?" Will asked, thinking fast.

"In my uncle's address book somewhere," Natasha said. "It's probably downstairs. Are you OK to walk?"

"Yes," Will grinned. *I know an erection can be debilitating in several ways, but I can still walk!*

"I'm so sorry to trail you up and downstairs," Natasha said, as they walked down. She placed a hand

115

on his lean, muscular back, feeling a spontaneous frisson of desire. "Especially when you're not feeling well. Listen – have you eaten recently?"

"No," Will admitted. Eating had been the last thing on his mind.

"Then no wonder you're feeling ill!" she cried. "Will you stay to dinner? I would honestly welcome the company – I don't actually know anyone here." She gazed imploringly at him. "You would be doing me a favor! And… in turn… I could maybe do y… do one for you!"

"OK," Will nodded, a cheeky grin creeping across his face.

"Great!" she smiled, her own mind working overtime. She had felt his powerful, muscular arms as she was helping him across the room. She was imagining them around her, or, better still, supporting his weight as he lay on top of her. She almost gasped, "We need to keep your strength up!" She gave him a pointed look, which even he could not mistake.

"I am all for that," he smiled. "Can I help you at all? Do anything… for you?"

She laughed. "Not just now. You relax. I make a mean Caesar salad," she said, crossing the kitchen to the small refrigerator.

"Great," Will said, grateful for anything. But most of all, he wanted the Grimoire Țepeș.

"Although, if you're really hungry," she said, her head in the fridge, "I also have a large steak we could share…" she brought out a plastic-wrapped plate. "Sometimes, a girl just needs a big hunk of meat."

"So I've heard," Will smirked, liking where this conversation was going. He stood up and headed towards her.

"Do you have a large…" Natasha turned around from the refrigerator, mischief written all over her face. "… appetite, Will?"

"Actually," he smiled, stepping forward and standing before her, within arm's reach. "I do have a large… appetite."

She took a step towards him. "Then I imagine I will have to satisfy it." She stood on tiptoes, and he leant down, so their lips touched tenderly.

She pulled away, a teasing look in her eyes. "You must be absolutely starving."

"In every way," he admitted.

***

After a fully satisfying evening, Will got dressed and ready to leave. Reluctantly, Natasha had got out of bed, dressed in a robe, and followed him downstairs.

"I *have* said you can stay," Natasha said plaintively. "Just for the night."

Will gave her a placatory peck on the lips. "I know. But I really have to go and finish what I've started. Find the book."

"Yes. I understand," Natasha's expression was wistful, but her tone was more resigned.

"But first, I need the address of this… Alison Smith?"

"I have her number here, anyway." She bustled over to a drawer, and flipped through the pages of an address book. "Oh. At least, I have the contact number of the university where she works… Shall we ring it?" she said hopefully. If there was no answer at this time of night, maybe Will would have no reason to rush off. He could stay with her.

Will frowned. "It's nearly 9pm. Is anyone likely to be there?"

"You never know," she said brightly, pressing the keys on the phone. She held the receiver to her ear, smiling, convinced that no one would pick up. Presumably

"Oh!" she exclaimed, her face falling, speaking into the phone. "Hello? I am seeking Alison Smith…" She paused, staring at Will's expectant face. She nodded, cast her glance down, said, "Uh-huh. Uh-huh. Oh. My late uncle – Herman Thayer – was a personal friend. I'm trying to contact her to inform her of his death and to locate some of his belongings in Ms Smith's possession. Yes, very close. Uh-huh…" She looked again at Will, nodded for a good minute and poised her pen over the book. "And do you have a contact number – or address?" She scribbled something down. "Thank you so much. No. That's great. Thank you. Goodbye."

Without saying a word to Will, she ripped a page out of the book.

"Apparently, she's on a sabbatical," Natasha explained. "Her colleague just happened to be working late in the office, and answered her phone. He doesn't have an address for her – and couldn't tell us such personal details, even if he did. However, he did say she has temporarily moved away with her husband, Donovan Smith, a property developer, who is doing some major rebuilding somewhere..." She glanced at the paper before handing it to him. "A place called Melas."

Wide-eyed, Will stared, aghast.

Natasha's brow furrowed in concern. "Are you OK, Will?"

"Yes," he croaked. "Gotta go!"

He rushed out of the front door, leaving Natasha hanging onto the doorframe, bewildered and bereft.

CHAPTER 8

Initially, Kate thought that it was her transformation into a vampire that had upset her system.

It must do, mustn't it? Being undead!

She had been feeling odd for weeks, but having never been a vampire before, she took it for granted that 'feeling odd' was the least of her worries.

Her periods had stopped, for example. *But then, being undead, maybe that's what happens,* she reasoned. She needed so much blood to drink, she had to hunt regularly for live humans to satisfy her craving. She was hardly likely to release more blood from her body, then – was she?

Is this what happens to young female vampires?

But who was she going to ask, for this intimate information? The arrogant Victor Rothenstein? Her post-menopausal mother, also newly 'turned' and therefore relatively inexperienced in vampire life?

Kate had initially thought that her feeling ill in the mornings was because she was unaccustomed to drinking large amounts of blood. Especially since she'd done it in the middle of the night, so feeling sick in the morning seemed likely. But it also happened even when she hadn't feasted on blood the night before.

Sickly nausea – in the mornings. Morning sickness. Periods stopped.

The thought crossed her mind: *If I weren't a vampire, I would think I was pregnant.*

Once the thought was in her head, she couldn't let it go. She tracked back her diary. She had been sleeping with William pretty much up to the point that she became a vampire. What if she'd got pregnant? Is that what had happened? It wasn't inconceivable – literally – for her, as a human, to be having Will's baby. So, then, as a vampire, was it possible?

Before she tortured herself any further with questions, she decided to sneak out one evening to pick up a pregnancy test kit. She couldn't go out herself in daylight, and she could hardly send her mother's PA out for it, could she? She needed to be certain whether she was pregnant or not, before she raised any alarms.

And now, sitting in the bathroom, watching the indicator of the white plastic stick she held in her fingers change color, she knew for sure. She was pregnant with William's baby!

Her heart was pounding, and she was breathless. She didn't know how she felt. Anxious and afraid. Excited and delighted. A thousand thoughts crossed her mind, simultaneously darting and weaving within the space of seconds. *Is this a vampire baby? What does that mean? Will it be normal? Will it survive? How can we bring it up, between the Darkness and the human world? Where is Will? Would he be happy? Could she keep this baby? Will it die, anyway?*

She allowed herself a moment to imagine an alternative universe, in which she and Will were together again – and none of this stuff had happened. If she wasn't a vampire. If she wasn't even Jackie Nixon's daughter. She imagined seeing Will's delight when she broke the news to him. *Daddy!* Both of them happy to be parents… married, even. Living together in their fairytale house, behind a white picket fence; bringing up their… daughter… or son. Happy ever after.

But that was fantasy. This was reality.

What am I gonna do? she wondered. *What would I do if I were still human?*

She still actually felt human – in part, at least. She had been afraid to admit it to her mother. Was that what the baby did to her? Helped her to retain some humanity in this madness of vampirism?

Kate sat and thought, carefully. She twisted the pregnancy test device in her hands, over and over. It was still true, no matter which way she looked at it. Besides, now she thought about it, she actually felt pregnant. She hadn't really needed this test to know it, but it had at least confirmed the fact.

She rested her hand on her belly, picturing the tiny scrap of life growing there. A part of herself, and a part of William. William, who had been an honourable and kind young man. A perfect boyfriend. If things had been different, she could have loved him. Longer. And now, this was all she had of her own in life and in love.

I want this baby, she decided. *My baby.*

She sat rocking ever so gently, her arms cradling her stomach, smiling.

My secret.
Not for long.

Even if she hid this knowledge from her mother and other people, she knew she couldn't do it forever – and that she would need somebody's help at some point. *The sooner the better!* She needed someone to put her mind at rest now, to be honest. Had any other vampire been in this situation? Were vampires ever born, as babies? Or were they made, as adults? What were the risks of having a baby, conceived as a human, now carried by a vampire mother? She needed to know.

She would have to tell her mother. And they would both have to glean as much knowledge of these matters as possible from Victor Rothenstein, with his centuries of experience as a vampire. Whatever happened, she wanted to safeguard this baby, and by her reckoning, she had fewer than eight months to figure it all out.

***

Kate had hoped that her mother would be pleased with the news. What she hadn't anticipated was her being absolutely wild with delight.

"This is perfect!" Jackie cried, clapping her hands with glee. She practically danced round the chamber in the Vampire Castle, grinning from ear to ear.

Jackie's happiness was infectious. Kate laughed in surprise. What a relief! She had been worrying so much, ever since she had suspected she might be pregnant. To know that she had her mother's immediate and unquestioning approval and support was more than she ever could have hoped for.

But Kate's relief was short-lived.

Jackie's eyes, which had been wide with excitement and happiness, suddenly narrowed in thought. "This can't happen soon enough, for me. In fact, I am sure I can find a spell to help to accelerate the baby's growth…"

"Why would I want to do that?" Kate frowned, unable to believe what she was hearing.

"It's not what *you* want that matters!" snapped Jackie. "I want the ancient sleep-lock opened, and the Vampire Army released. The faster we do that, the better!"

"I don't understand," muttered Kate in bewilderment. "What's that got to do with my baby?"

Jackie roared with laughter, tossing back her head, her throat straining. She laughed for thirty long seconds, straight, gasping for breath. It was such loud, maniacal laughter that Kate stood appalled, wondering if her mother had completely lost her mind.

"Ooof!" Jackie exhaled, one hand delicately on her chest. She was panting as if recovering from some long physical exertion. Grinning, she shook her head in disbelief. "Oh, Kate. You do make me laugh! It has EVERYTHING to do with 'your' baby, of course!"

Kate's facial expression was the very definition of confusion.

Rolling her eyes in irritation, Jackie explained, "We just need to sacrifice the baby to open the sleep-lock!" She threw her arms in the air in delight.

Kate's face crumpled in horror and disgust. "What?"

"This is ideal!" Jackie was chuckling happily to herself. "And there I was, thinking we would have to raid some maternity hospital for a newborn when the time came, but – this couldn't be better!" Wildly, her eyes swiveled from side to side, imagining the scenario, and already making plans.

"NO!" Kate yelled. "You are not killing my baby!"

"Ridiculous, Kate," her mother scoffed. "It's just a means to an end." Her eyes gleamed, and she smiled at the thought of what she would achieve when the legions of vampires were reawakened.

"NO!" Kate's voice rose to shrill hysteria. "I won't let you! You won't!"

Jackie slapped her daughter hard across the face, her head jerking back on her neck with a crack, from the force of the blow. Her skin stung, and her ears rang. She stood blinking blankly, waiting for the swirling stars she was seeing to disappear, trying to take in what was happening.

"Don't get attached!" Jackie spat, her eyes bulging with fury. "The child is mine, and it *will* be sacrificed!"

"Oh, no, Mother!" Kate screamed. "No way! You're not using MY baby!" Kate gave a guttural roar of rage, raised her arms and lunged forward, her hands like claws, aiming to throttle Jackie.

With a single lift of her palm, Jackie stopped Kate in her tracks. She froze in mid-air for a second, a look of shock and distress on her face, before her body crumpled into a heap on the floor.

"Watch you don't damage that baby," sneered Jackie, standing over her daughter's limp, almost lifeless body. "I need it."

Beneath Jackie's smug gaze, Kate lay on her side with her eyes closed, breathing deeply, a soft sniffle occasionally escaping from her like a snore.

"I knew that 'sleeping beauty' spell would come in handy one day," Jackie said aloud, with satisfaction.

She walked towards the open door. "Guards!"

Two pale demon guards stepped from their positions either side of the threshold and stood to attention.

"My daughter is a little tired. Take her to her bedroom and place her on the bed. Secure the room. She may be asleep for some time."

The guards bent down and awkwardly hoisted up Kate's body, her arms dangling limply as they carried her out of the door.

Standing alone in the empty castle chamber, Jackie could not contain her excitement. Her grin simply became wider, and as incongruous as the gesture was, for a middle-aged vampire in an evening gown, she punched the air in victory.

Jackie knew that she could now start making preparations to sacrifice Kate's child as soon as it was born. And she couldn't wait to boast. She would take great delight in rubbing the news in Victor's face and hurried along the corridor to the guarded room in which she would find the captive vampire.

She walked into Victor's prison room, beaming. "My plans move apace!"

Sitting on the dusty floor with his back against the wall, Victor raised his head, interested despite himself.

Jackie gleefully explained her news. "And using my acceleration spell on the thing's growth, I will very shortly be even more powerful…"

Victor actually felt physically sick. This was worse than even he had imagined. That she would sacrifice her own grandchild without a qualm!

Jackie's eyes gleamed madly. "Prepare for earth-shattering changes, when I finally open the sleep-lock and assume leadership of my legions of vampires! Cower before me – fools!"

Victor was aghast. *She is completely crazed with power!*

***

Marlon Coldbridge was the detective conducting the investigation into Alison Smith's disappearance, and he wasn't too happy. He had interviewed the missing woman's husband, Donovan Smith, on a couple of occasions already – and despite Don telephoning the office every day demanding news and action, giving the appearance of the devoted husband, Marlon remained unconvinced.

There was just something about Don Smith that raised a red flag, for the detective.

The first interview had been fairly straightforward – Don had contacted the police and filed a missing person's report within sixteen hours. But for a grown adult to be missing, that was no time. The police had assured him that they couldn't investigate until Alison had been missing for longer. Yet he was adamant that they should do something straight away.

The next interview was a little more searching; required more facts and a detailed statement.

Coldbridge had asked a perfectly reasonable, straightforward question. "Where were you on the night of your wife's disappearance?"

"A business meeting," Don said vaguely.

When pressed for more detail, he had told Detective Coldbridge that he had to keep the identity of the client confidential. It was a sensitive business negotiation, and the client would be incensed – would definitely withdraw from the deal – and potentially ruin Don's company if his identity were revealed, or if he became embroiled in a police investigation.

Coldbridge stared at him blankly. *The guy keeps evading the questions.*

He had observed Don's earnest desperation, and the cold sweat that broke out on his forehead and upper lip. Classic tells. The detective was suspicious that Don knew more than he was telling.

And now, Marlon Coldbridge was back again at Don's place of work, on the case, and had spent another hour with Don. He had got no further than before. He had just reminded Don again that his police colleagues had questioned him about the deaths of the town's reconstruction workers and he had also been the prime witness of the death of his business partner, Mike Moran.

"Can you see the common denominator, Mr. Smith?" Marlon asked.

Don lifted his head and gazed sorrowfully at the detective. "I know how it looks."

"The story you told about your partner's death…" the detective paused for effect, and consulted his notes. "And I quote: 'Huge bats the size of a man'… Sounds pretty incredible. Wouldn't you agree?"

Don cradled his forehead in one hand, and mumbled, "Yes. Yes. It does sound incredible. But I can only tell you what I saw."

"Hmmm," Detective Coldbridge considered. "Anything more to add? Anything else you've remembered?"

Don shook his head, defeated. This was his worst nightmare.

"Well," Coldbridge said grimly, placing his notes in his messenger bag and standing up. He opened the office door, turned back around and said wryly, "Thank you. You've been very helpful. Again."

As he closed the door behind him, the secretary raised her eyebrows and stared at him questioningly. He didn't like to encourage her potential gossip, so set off across the room.

"Detective!" the secretary said with emphasis, although she was trying to keep her voice low, for some reason. She scurried over to him, her high heels clicking on the linoleum.

Glancing over her shoulder to ensure that Don was still firmly ensconced in his office, she muttered urgently, "I'm sure Don won't have said… but… did you know? People say he's having an affair?"

Coldbridge's interest was piqued. "Tell me more."

"Could just be a rumor…" the woman said doubtfully. "But – seems like it could be with Jackie Nixon."

Coldbridge nodded encouragingly. "Anything else?"

She shrugged. "I just thought you should know. With Alison going missing and all. You know. Besides, maybe Jackie Nixon might know something."

Coldbridge nodded, and smiled briskly. "Well, thank you, ma'am. You've been most helpful."

With his quick mind making calculations as a result of this new information, he rushed to his car to share his findings with his colleagues.

***

Will used his time and the quietness of the flight to make a connection with Victor Rothenstein. He had rarely attempted to activate the vampire communication spell, because the feeling of having the vampire in his head actually made him feel ill. He had never experienced such evil – not even when he was battling with powerful demons. At least their wickedness and sin wasn't under his skin, then.

But, like a psychic telephone, Will felt that he definitely needed to tell Victor his news – the fact that he wasn't yet in possession of the Grimoire Ţepeş. But that remarkably, it was actually already in Melas, so he was very hopeful that he would get his hands on it soon.

But when Will decided to sit in peaceful meditation and reach out to Victor, his plans to reveal his discoveries were completely railroaded by Victor's urgent voice in his head.

"William! We have an emergency situation!"

"What?" Will said, in his mind. In real life, his brow furrowed.

"Jackie is preparing for the ritual to unlock the sleep-lock…" Victor said. "The most vital element of this specific ritual is the sacrifice of a newborn baby…"

"Again?" Will said, horrified. He had already witnessed such a ritual – when Jackie Nixon had sacrificed Will's own baby cousin to open the portal to the Darkness.

"But listen carefully, Will," Victor said. "She has her eye set on a very specific newborn. Kate is pregnant and is carrying your baby…"

Will's mind leapt in a confusion of thoughts.

"Mine?" he breathed. He couldn't take this all in. *Kate is having a baby? And it is mine? I'm going to be a father?* This was confusing enough – panic and shock coupled with a smidgeon of delight and excitement. But all of this was overshadowed with the utter horror of what Victor had previously told him. *Jackie is going to sacrifice my child, too?*

A roar of rage almost escaped Will's lips, even where he sat on the airplane. He actually stood up suddenly, looking round wildly, as if he might get off the plane there and then to do something. The passengers beside him looked up in alarm. Will was totally dumbfounded by this discovery – and felt helpless and useless. He sat down, exasperated.

Victor's voice interrupted. "Kate's now her mother's prisoner."

Will couldn't think, let alone speak. He had no idea what Victor might be picking up via the communication channel between them. A mess of emotion.

But Victor carried on, regardless. "We need to do something – and fast. Jackie is so keen for a quick resolution, she is accelerating the child's growth so it'll be ready in time for the winter solstice."

Will's mind reeled. Winter solstice? The middle of December? Just a couple of months away? His unease and anger turned into a creeping venom.

During the conversation, because of the power of the communication spell's linkage between Will and Victor, Will could sense Victor's evil nature so strongly while they communicated, that he actually felt that it was part of himself. He fully experienced the unspeakable evil radiating from the vampire. Not only could he feel it, but it consumed all of his senses and filled his mind, making his skin crawl.

The evil was within Will. Will was the evil.

PART 2

BELLA

CHAPTER 9

Goth Rock diva Bella Howard looked in the mirror and pressed both hands to her pale, sweat-clammy cheeks.

"Fucksake," she croaked aloud, taking in crumbling mascara caked on her lashes in clods; the staining from rivulets of old black eyeliner; the smudged black lips and the grey skin pitted with old foundation. Or the remains of it. Somewhere, she had cast aside her black tailcoat and crushed velvet top hat. But otherwise, she was still wearing the remains of last night's stage costume: a frothy ruffled white shirt, now stained with alcohol, and a long black ballerina's tutu over striped stockings and high laced boots. *I slept with my boots on?* Along with the grotesque mask of decaying makeup that cracked her face, she looked like she was wearing a Halloween costume. Except Halloween was weeks away.

She gently prodded one of the dark, puffy shadows under her eyes.

Something dead, she decided. *I look dead. Like someone's attacked me and I've been murdered.*

Her long ash-blonde hair was a bird's nest of tangles and split ends. She raked her red fingernails through it, trying to make some improvement. Unsuccessfully.

Inside her throat felt raw. She pressed her fingers to her neck, experimentally, expecting to feel it bruised. *Did someone try to throttle me?*

Was she getting a cold? Laryngitis? The singer's nightmare!

Have I been throwing up? She couldn't remember the night before, as usual, but she felt a scalded sensation at the back of her mouth, as if she had been puking up stomach acid and bile. She swallowed, and her throat burned. Maybe she had vomited at some point. She just couldn't remember anything – not even the gig. She was so out of it the night before.

She groaned. Talk about living the dream. She was living up to the reputation she had developed – the persona she presented as lead vocalist of the band Belladonna Rose. The hard rocking, coke-snorting, hard drinking, sexually promiscuous, hard living stage-Bella herself. She was a hard act to follow. And to live up to. Even for herself.

The other members of the band – Lex Wilde, Ash Abs, Cassie Dean – were no saints, either. Give them freedom, give them money, give them drugs and alcohol, and they were maniacs. They were all really bad for one another, but together, as a band – they were so good. Bella was caught in an impossible situation.

Victims of our own success.

She gazed down at her pale hands, uncontrollably trembling with delirium tremens as she came down from the alcohol and drugs. *What a mess!* And the only thing that would help would be another slug of the absinthe she favored. Or as she preferred to call it, "*la fée verte*" – the green fairy. She loved the ritual of pouring the strong, ethereally pale green liquor into her special cut-crystal absinthe glass, then pouring water over a specially-designed straining spoon nestling a sugar lump within its hollow, and watching the liquor turn cloudy, like a magic potion. But that reverential ritual was only for when she was relatively sober. Or when she got someone else to do it for her. She had no patience at all for that when she was drunk. As much booze, as fast as possible, was the key. And any liquor would do, then. Or coke. Or meth. Or dope. Failing that, a handful of benzos like xanax, valium, ativan, or klonopin – or whatever other uppers she could get her hands on. There was nothing she hadn't tried. Nothing she wasn't tired of.

Bella groaned again, sticking out her tongue, observing its coating of white fur, while straining in the mirror to see down the darkness of her raw, sore throat. With her pounding head and cold sweat, she was wrecked.

I'm nearly dead. If I'm not careful, I will be.

Belladonna Rose's latest album 'Bloodsucker' had already sold 10 million copies, but lead singer Bella Howard was close to having a nervous breakdown from an overdose of sex, drugs, and rock 'n roll.

I need a major detox.

***

Allowed into the house by one of the servants, Detective Marlon Coldbridge took in the atmosphere of the house as he walked through. For the newly-built home of an extremely wealthy woman, it was a strange, cold and dark place – with little character and personality. It almost had the feeling of a holiday let, temporary accommodation where people spent little time, rather than a homely, luxurious place that was their main abode. He understood that Jackie Nixon had some kind of extreme allergy to sunlight, but if she couldn't leave the house much – wouldn't you think it would be less clinical? More comfortable?

Her PA had sat him in a clinical anteroom, very sparsely furnished, saying, "Ms Nixon will see you shortly."

But Coldbridge, left alone, had an unaccountably uneasy feeling in that place. From the corner of his eye, while he was waiting to be summoned, he kept catching a glimpse of a tall, pale gray figure. But it couldn't be. Because every time he turned to look, there was no one there. Alert, all his senses were tuned into making some kind of logical sense out of this. The place was brand new, and in pristine condition. It wasn't like it was a creepy old haunted house, and yet... It had that vibe.

There it was again!

A pale gray blur, just in his peripheral vision. And yet, at the same time, it wasn't. Once his attention was drawn to the spot where he'd seen the figure – as soon as he looked – it was gone. Had it vanished? Or was it never there at all?

He rubbed his eyes once again. He made a mental note to make an appointment with the optometrist to get his eyes tested. This was crazy.

Jackie Nixon's PA appeared again. Not from the direction he had last seen the illusory gray figure, but quite the opposite – so there was no mistaking her for what he had seen. If he had, indeed, seen anything. Besides, she was wearing a black suit, and was petite. Not a tall, pale gray figure that suggested a male presence.

A presence? he pulled himself up fast. *What the hell am I thinking? I'm seeing a ghost?*

"Ms Nixon will see you now," the PA smiled. But it was a very professional, cold smile, Coldbridge noticed.

"Great," he said, standing up to follow her, shaking off his doubts and becoming the all-professional police detective again.

Coldbridge strode confidently into Jackie Nixon's dimly lit, shaded room to interview her.

Jackie Nixon immediately sat up and took notice. Not because he was a police officer, or an authority figure, but because his rugged good looks and powerful, muscular frame had got Jackie Nixon's juices flowing at first sight. She sprang up, deftly opening the top button of her V-necked blouse at the same time, to reveal more cleavage.

"Ms Nixon? Detective Coldbridge," he extended his hand to shake Jackie's.

She stood overly close to him – well within his own personal space. She was holding onto his hand for far too long for his comfort, too.

"Detective…" One of her hands slid up his arm and squeezed his bulging bicep appreciatively. "Let's not stand on ceremony…" She oozed seduction, gazing at him with half-closed eyes. "Do call me Jackie. And you are…?"

"Detective Coldbridge," he stated again, extricating himself from her grasp. The woman was nothing, if not obvious!

Jackie laughed, a pretentious tinkling laugh. "Do take a seat, *Detective Coldbridge!*"

He sat down on the leather couch across the room from where she had been sitting previously, but she followed him, panther-like, and decoratively arranged herself beside him, their thighs almost touching.

"And *what... exactly...* can I *do* for you, Detective?" she emphasised breathily, leaning forward so that the globes of her enhanced breasts were more visible over the gaping opening of her blouse.

"As I mentioned on the phone," Coldbridge began, "I have a few questions for you. Regarding your relationship with Donovan Smith."

Jackie arched her eyebrows in wonder. "Relationship? Any reputation I have with Mr Smith is purely professional. My company has contracted with his company to develop the Melas town site."

"*Purely* professional?" Coldbridge stared her right in the eyes, challenging her to lie.

"In the sense that I pay him for his services..." Jackie laughed again. "...in construction." She placed a hand mid-way up Coldbridge's thigh, and squeezed it. "Not for his... erections, in the sense you mean, *Detective*."

Coldbridge stood up, glaring at her. "And beyond the business of the Melas site, or any of the construction company business – have you ever met up with Donovan Smith socially? As a friend – of any description?"

140

Jackie rolled her eyes upwards, as if in thought. "Let me see…" She let the tip of her tongue protrude from her red-painted pout, and, watching Coldbridge staring at her, ensuring that she had his full attention, she licked her lips slowly, making him wait. "No. Can't say that I have. I don't like to mix business with *pleasure*."

She stood up and stepped forward, only a couple of inches from Coldbridge. "Let us never, ever, do any business together, Detective." She leant forward, so her breasts pressed against his ribs, and he could smell her breath, which exuded a scent of sexual excitement. "Then, the *pleasure* will be all ours."

Coldbridge stepped away from her. Out of the corner of his eye, he was convinced he saw another glimpse of that strange pale figure. It was unnerving him, but he maintained his composure. Jackie Nixon was lying, he was convinced, but he had no proof. He could only ask again, "So you deny having any kind of personal relationship with Donovan Smith?"

"Oh," Jackie said teasingly, one fingernail pressed to her lower lip, her eyes wide and innocent. "I never usually *deny myself* anything… usually." She shrugged. "But in this case – yes. I deny having anything but a professional relationship with Mr Smith."

Coldbridge stared coldly into her lying eyes. "Then I won't waste any more of your valuable time, Ms Nixon. Thank you."

Just as he turned to go, Jackie grasped his huge bicep once again and stopped him. He stared down at her amused expression.

141

She shook her head as if in disbelief and said, "He's a construction worker, for fucksake. Hardly in my league."

When Marlon Coldbridge stepped out into the fresh air, he was relieved to have escaped that house.

Gives me the creeps! he shuddered. *And as for that bloody woman... She's fobbed me off with lies. Fuck her. And not in the way she clearly wants me to.*

***

Belladonna Rose was playing a night in Morgantown, West Virginia, on their 'Bloodsucker' North American tour. This was practically home turf for Bella Howard, and she was unusually alone, resting in her five-star hotel room before she had to go over for the sound-checks. She flung herself onto the luxurious bed, took a drag of her spliff and reached for her habitual glass of absinthe and water. Smiling hazily, the drink and the drugs already taking effect, she switched on the TV remote and the local news suddenly burst into life on the screen. Not normally one to watch TV news, she sat sipping her drink nevertheless, curious to hear whether or not they would mention any familiar places from her childhood and teenage years.

A man's face filled the screen.

Bella almost choked up the mouthful of absinthe – the bitter taste of wormwood flooding back over her tongue.

Don?

She clattered down her precious crystal glass onto the bedside table, and crawled forward on the bed,

142

squinting, trying to get a better view of the face and words on the widescreen TV.

The banner at the bottom of the screen read: '*Donovan Smith; Director: Moran-Smith Construction*'.

It IS Don Smith!

Don Smith, her childhood sweetheart, her first love! He was there on TV – his face filling all 50 wide inches of the giant flat screen! Looking desperately serious and concerned, and decades older, but still the handsome-featured man she had once loved. What was going on?

Amazed, she turned up the volume.

"And when did you last see your missing wife?" asked the presenter, off-screen.

Donovan's face crumpled. "It's been well over a week… at our home, close by the Melas site…"

"Which is the development your company, Moran-Smith, is working on, currently…" said the disembodied voice of the presenter.

The camera was fixed on a close-up of Don's face, every crease and line of age and anxiety visible in HD. Bella could even see the individual spikes of graying stubble on his face. But those blue eyes were the killer. So pained and troubled. They pierced Bella's heart, despite the dulling effect of the drink and drugs.

"The same site where several people have been found mysteriously killed – including your business partner, Mike Moran?"

"Well… that wasn't actually Melas…" Don said warily.

"But near enough? Within five miles?"

"Yes," murmured Don. "Yes…"

"Our roving reporter, Travis Bendt, speaking today to businessman Donovan Smith, whose wife has gone missing, in the town of Melas, there…" The scene switched back to the studio, a blonde news anchor beaming, before changing the subject entirely.

Don Smith!

Seeing Donovan Smith on TV, it brought back better times for Bella. Don was always so kind, so caring. But she had outgrown him and become wild. What would life have been like, if she had married her high school sweetheart? *Boring,* she thought. But frankly, she was tired out, now. She no longer wanted to be a wild child. At least, not for a while. She could use some boring stability. She could use an old friend who knew her as small-town girl Isabella Howard. Someone she could be herself with.

Myself? she wondered. *Who am I?*

She used to be loving and caring towards Don – as he was to her, back in those days of innocence. Looked like he needed a friend, too, just now. Maybe they could help one another. At least, till his wife turned up.

Sex was the last thing on her mind, she surprised herself by thinking. She'd had her fill of sex to last a lifetime. But Don was reliable and steady and caring – just what she needed just now, and he looked to be in trouble. She couldn't do much, but maybe she could offer him the hand of friendship again. And, just returning to a childhood friendship was just what she needed now – a reprieve from the pressure; a respite from the stress of being in a non-stop hamster wheel of frenzied partying and performing.

Bella immediately called up the TV station, who gave her a telephone number for Don's business, at least. Pulling her weight as a local and national celebrity, she managed to persuade his secretary to see if she would be allowed his number. The secretary quickly called and checked with Don. Within minutes, Bella was able to ring through to Don's personal cell-phone.

"Bella?" Don gasped in disbelief. "Bella Howard! It must be – what? Twenty years?"

"Less! Don't make me out to be so old, Don!" she said sadly. "God, talking to you takes me back. I wish I was that young again. I can't tell you…"

Don's voice was wistful, too, "Oh, Bella."

Bella commiserated with Don over Alison, and his recent troubles, and Don suddenly found himself feeling unburdened. Except for the unsympathetic Mike and the cold Jackie, he had had no one to confide in, no one to even talk to, apart from police and news reporters – who were hardly likely to comfort him. Bella listened without judging, and offered him the first support he felt he'd had since this whole horrible affair began. He was so grateful, he could have cried.

"Hey, Don – I can't imagine what you're going through, there," Bella admitted, her voice lowering to a whisper. "I really do feel your pain. I'm going through some tough times myself…"

"You?" Don asked in surprise. "Successful – rich – what's not to love?"

Bella's voice cracked with emotion. "Don… I… sometimes… I think I'm losing it. I can't take the stress… the pressure. You don't know…"

"Tell me, babe."

Babe. The word took her straight back to being fourteen again. Arm in arm with everybody's high school football hero: Donovan Smith. It was a warm and comforting feeling.

They chatted a while longer, Don's soft tones soothing her, and her uplifting optimism about Alison rallying his own spirits.

"We're just playing in Morgantown tonight, then – thank fuck – we have a couple of days' break before we move on to Charlotte…"

"Hey, you're not far from me. Why don't you come down to Melas?" Don said. "It would be great to see you!"

Bella hesitated. Her heart had soared at the thought of catching up with Don, but… "There are the other guys to think about. The rest of the band."

"All of you, come!" Don laughed, gratified to have something to think about, to take him out of himself and his funk. His worries about Alison.

Bella laughed, picturing the guys in a small town in West Virginia. Their floor-length black leather trenchcoats, their eyeliner, their biker boots, their funeral directors' top hats and Cassie's red plaid miniskirts with a back bustle made of yards of black tulle netting.

It would be fun to wipe off all her stage makeup, uncover the freckles. Did she still have freckles? It had been so long since she'd let her skin breathe. Wear a pair of jeans and a gingham top. Or a hoodie and sneakers. It would be like playing dress-up. Like touching the past. Getting back to her roots.

Yeah. The more she thought about it, the more a weekend off in a place like Melas was very appealing.

"But don't expect too much excitement here," Don warned.

Bella laughed wryly. "Trust me. The last thing I want is excitement."

"Then you'll be in the right place," Don said. "You and the band come to Melas for a quiet weekend."

"Sounds like bliss."

CHAPTER 10

Detective Marlon Coldbridge couldn't settle. That afternoon had only confirmed to him that Jackie Nixon was implicated in these strange occurrences. After he left Jackie Nixon's strangely shrouded dark house, he had telephoned Donovan Smith's secretary right away to invite her to meet with him after work for more questions. When he interviewed her that evening, to see if he could find out any actual facts, she wasn't able to give many more details. But she was convinced, herself, from the number of times she had seen Jackie and Don together that there was something going on.

"Everyone says so," she told him.

When he had pressed her for the specific names of 'everyone,' she hadn't been able to say for sure. A couple of the guys onsite had just nodded and grinned when she had mentioned her suspicions. But Coldbridge got the impression that she was the only one given to gossip. She was the only woman, and he tried to suppress his tendency to think that women were more interested in this kind of thing: spotting signs of romance. He noted down the names of the guys, planning to speak to them the next day.

But the secretary was convinced. The evidence she gave was Jackie's flirtatious manner and Don's evident acceptance of it.

She sure is sexually-motivated, Coldbridge thought. *Threw herself at me. If she tried that with Donovan Smith – how hard would it be to resist, when she's a wealthy client and a powerful woman? Imagine doing business with her, having to fend her off every day and trying not to insult her by rejecting her advances.*

The more Coldbridge thought about it, the more he thought the man would either have to be a saint, or completely careless of his company's future, to resist Jackie Nixon if she had her heart set on him – or her claws into him.

The secretary continued: "Also, the number of appointments Don has with her – he meets with her far more than any other client, normally. He always told me he was never to be disturbed while he was with her. Even if his wife called urgently. It all adds up."

An affair was the only logical conclusion.

"And his wife, Alison," Coldbridge had asked. "Do you think she had any idea?"

Don's secretary shrugged. "I really don't know, Detective. She almost never came to the office, and I know Don said she was really busy writing some book…"

"Book?" Coldbridge asked with interest. "What kind of book?"

"Oh, you know – one of these academic things to do with her specialism… paranormal stuff. Ghosts or something."

Ghosts? Coldbridge sat up with a start, but recovered his composure. He had almost forgotten about the strange feeling he had had in Jackie Nixon's house, and the glimpses he caught from the corner of his eyes, as if there was a pale ghostly figure passing by, or watching somewhere. And the fact that he could never be sure what he saw, because the figure always vanished.

In spite of himself, a shiver rippled up Coldbridge's spine, and he felt the hairs on the back of his neck stand on end.

Like a dog with its hackles up, Coldbridge thought. That's always what he felt when he was onto something. And there was something about Jackie Nixon and that house, that he was sure held the answers.

As an ex-Marine and a law-enforcement officer for many years, he had learned to trust his intuition. And after all, his intuition had kept him alive this long.

But he had nothing to go on. No facts. No evidence. Just a gut instinct, and that weird feeling and half-sightings of something strange in the old Madison House, where Jackie now lived.

Nothing to warrant investigation, *if it was done by the book*. Nothing to even allow him to get a search warrant granted. There was no proof of any misconduct or suspicion, and Jackie was highly respected and politically connected. For Coldbridge to suggest that he needed to search her house, or point the finger of blame in her direction at all – even as an accomplice, or as the reason for Don killing his own wife, or for Alison running away – it would be an uphill battle. Coldbridge wasn't at all sure he could get his superiors, the sheriff, the local mayor or, heck, even the governor for that matter, to allow him to prod further into Jackie's affairs.

Affairs! He almost laughed, wryly.

But he just knew, in his soul, that he had to find out more – and that house was the key.

He had wracked his brain trying to think of a legal approach, but it came to nothing. There was nothing else for it, then. He had acted on a hunch many times before, and it had always come good.

Which is why 2 a.m. found him breaking into the Madison House to investigate further.

Even if he found anything, he knew it was inadmissible evidence, obtained illegally. But if he did find something, it could give him the incentive to drive forward with his legal investigation. And the proof that he was doing the right thing.

He had scoped out the place already that day. No evident burglar alarm, which surprised him. But maybe Jackie felt it unnecessary, since the construction site her property was on was so heavily guarded, that it was almost a gated community of her own. She had even mentioned – pointedly – that her staff all left soon after darkness fell. She lived alone with her daughter, whom she said was rarely there.

"There's just little old me, rattling about all alone in this big house. It gets so-o-o-o lonely," Jackie had breathed heavily, staring into his eyes with obvious meaning. "I can't tell you how wonderful it would be to spend the night with a strapping, handsome man to look after me." And she had squeezed his muscular arm again.

151

Marlon Coldbridge had it all worked out. If he was caught, he could come up with some elaborate story for Jackie – saying that he had read the signals she gave out that day. Telling her that he wanted to give her a frisson of excitement by suddenly appearing in her bedroom in the dead of night. That he thought she looked like the type of woman who would adore spontaneity – a little danger, even. That he had been trying to maintain a professional front, but just couldn't wait any longer, and he was a man who acted on instinct when he was faced with an amazing woman. He thought she might fall for that kind of line. She appeared to have an ego huge enough to believe that all men would find her irresistible.

Coldbridge placed his hand on the front door handle before taking out his lock-picking set, which was in his pocket. To his surprise and relief, the handle turned easily and opened the door. Unlocked! He couldn't believe his luck. He wouldn't even have to break in.

The hallway was even blacker than its dimness during the day, and as he closed the door quietly behind him, his eyes strained to accustom themselves to this level of darkness. He took out his small Maglite and clicked it on, its narrow beam picking out the sparse detail he recalled from earlier, that afternoon.

Where first? he wondered. He hadn't seen anything suspicious in the living room. The kitchen – as a last resort. He wasn't sure what he was looking for – love letters from Don? Some signs of Alison? But if he started on the first floor and worked his way up... maybe he would come across something – like a study – that might contain some evidence.

But before he had a chance to tiptoe down the hallway and try a door, in a split-second of awareness that reminded him of the half-caught glimpses he had seen earlier that day, he was suddenly and violently side-swiped by a flurry of pale gray movement and heavy muscle. It flung him sideways and pinned him to the ground, all red flashing eyes and snarling teeth that took his breath away.

His eyes wide, Coldbridge stared in shock and horror at the beast lying on top and above him – all scaly skin and ravening jaws, frothing at the mouth like a rabid dog.

"Ah. You met one of my demon guards," came a voice somewhere in the dark above him. A dim light clicked on, making Coldbridge squint.

It was Jackie, her eyes wild and furious and her hair flaming.

"You sickening fool!" she roared, and fell upon Coldbridge's throat, as the demon guard swiftly and deftly moved out of her way.

She sank her fangs deep into the skin of his neck, and Coldbridge was frozen in a paroxysm of pure terror. Jackie sucked powerfully on the wound she had made, summoning the liquid of life from his his blood vessels. Coldbridge actually felt his blood drawn strongly back against nature, irresistibly moving through his artery and veins, pumping into her mouth. For a glorious few seconds, he actually felt a thrill of sexual passion, like an orgasm, but that was short-lived. As was he.

Jackie drank deeply of the detective's blood till he breathed his last and died with a gentle sigh.

Jackie got up, and stood over Marlon Coldbridge's still-warm body. Her eyes traced down from his pale and stricken, rugged face, to his broad shoulders. *Those huge biceps!*

His blood-stained shirt strained over his broad chest, well-defined with muscle.

"What a goddamned waste," she tutted, her lip quirking into a sneer.

She was half-tempted to unzip his trousers and see what she had missed. But what was the point? That was no use to her now.

She turned away in disgust.

"Dispose of the body in the Darkness," she instructed the pale demon guards.

***

On Friday, the Goth Rock band Belladonna Rose's huge tour bus pulled up in Melas just inside the construction area, and Bella Howard led the rest of the way on foot to the site office, where she had arranged to meet Donovan Smith whenever they arrived in town.

The band arrived in Melas looking like an anachronism – their dark Victorian urban fantasy clothing at odds with the West Virginian small town. As well as her fellow band members, Bella had also brought over her closest friend, Romeo Luiz, a Brazilian warlock and mystic. He was traveling on this leg of the tour with them.

The guys all wore black skinny jeans and studded leather jackets, looking lean and mean, only differentiated from a distance by their hair. Keyboardist

Lex Wilde's massive black curly Afro that always gave him the appearance of a dandelion seed-head ball and emphasized the stark white of his skin, contrasted with Drummer Ash Abs' long black hair, dragged back in a ponytail. Romeo Luiz was dark-skinned with long braided hair that spread across his shoulders in bunched dreadlocks.

Most of the town was still under construction, so their black biker boots and silver buckles were soon muddied. Cassie Dean, the female lead guitar player of the band, tentatively picked her way across the sandy road in her high heeled button-boots, her long black velvet skirts held in her hand. Construction workers in plaid shirts, jeans and hard hats stopped what they were doing and stared at the motley crew.

"Fuckin' Rednecks!" Cassie muttered. "Shit, Bella – where the hell you brung us, girl?" she complained.

Bella laughed. "On an adventure!"

Bella herself had dressed to kill. She wore a deeply-cut black crushed velvet Victorian style dress with voluminous mutton-sleeves and frothy underskirts, which she held bunched up in her fists as she tiptoed through the mud. The low neckline and tightly laced corset bodice of the dress emphasized the expanse of her creamy-white cleavage that jiggled like barely-set jello as she moved. She had taken great care with her makeup and costume – more care than she did before going on stage, frankly, because she was meeting her first love, Don. No woman wants to meet an ex unless she looks a million dollars, and Bella was no exception.

He might be married, and he might be bereft because his wife's missing, but I still want him to know

155

what he's missing! she thought, as she headed across the muddy rutted road, her sights set on the temporary office – a large metal hut. She found her heart beating with excitement at the prospect of seeing Don again in the flesh for the first time in almost twenty years. Their long telephone conversation had been intimate and comforting, and had brought all those old feelings of love flooding back.

Donovan Smith wasn't the only attraction for Bella Howard. When Don had been telling her about his recent situation and work – the massive contract he was working on for Jackie Nixon – just hearing about the wealthy and powerful Jackie Nixon had piqued Bella's interest, too.

Maybe I should get into property development, Bella thought. *Maybe invest my money instead of spending it all on booze and coke.*

"I'd love to meet this woman," Bella said. "If we come to Melas, can you fix for us to meet her?"

Don's blood had run cold at the thought. After her recent revelations, Don had no intention of going anywhere near Jackie Nixon for a long, long time if he could avoid it.

"Um… I don't know. She's a really busy woman…" he had blustered, eventually fudging the issue with a reluctant, "Maybe."

He hoped Bella would completely forget about Jackie. If he could keep her busy and entertained, maybe she wouldn't bring her up again. Trouble was, there wasn't that much to do in Melas. They had barely brought a tenth of it back to life, so he would have to take them out of town if they wanted any fun. Bella had assured him that she wanted a weekend of relaxation, catching up with an old friend, but as for her band, crew and entourage – that was another matter.

"Don!" Bella burst into the site management hut, her arms wide open, and hurtled towards him to embrace him.

The first thing that struck him – visually as well as physically – was her ample bosom, wobbling towards him, looking altogether larger because of her tiny cinched waist and the massive uplift that the corset gave to her breasts. From his reckoning, these breasts were natural, unlike Jackie Nixon's surgically enhanced ones that stayed immobile and perky on her chest like small hard hats, even when she was lying down.

My! Bella's grown! She was certainly no longer the skinny kid he'd known. She had filled out, but he must admit – it was for the better. *Womanly.*

"Bella!" he cried, delighted to see her again. He folded his arms around her, acutely conscious of her soft breasts pressed against his ribcage. He buried his face in her fragrant blonde hair, and felt an unexpected stirring in his loins. He remembered how well their bodies fitted together – like matching pieces of the same jigsaw. How often they had walked about with their arms around one another, simply happy to be together. He couldn't remember the last time he had walked anywhere with his arm around Alison's shoulder, with her tucked into his side, molding to his body, her own arm around his waist. And now Jackie had revealed the truth, Don knew that he never would, again.

He had a flashback to his youth: those times of making out with Isabella Howard, during their slow, innocent courtship over the couple of years they had been together. How voraciously hungry and exploratory they had been when they first made love. And that's what it had been for him: pure love. Unlike other good-looking teenage boys, he really wasn't just after sex. He had given himself to Bella first, to demonstrate only to her the depths of his love and caring for her. He'd been in it for the long haul. But... somehow, she had outgrown him.

Lost in memories, he opened his eyes and suddenly realized that a crowd of black-clad eccentric characters had followed Bella into the office, too, and stood looking shifty and slightly bewildered to witness such an extended physical greeting between their lead singer and some guy they'd never seen before. Don recognized them as the band, of course, from their TV appearances and videos, although he wasn't really a fan of that type of music. He had always maintained an idle interest and a secret pride in what Bella had achieved, however.

Bella laughed, and introduced Don to them all, ending with: "And this is my good friend, Romeo Luiz."

The striking Brazilian stepped forward, fixing Don with an intensely sharp and persistent stare. He extended his elegant brown hand towards Don in a gesture that seemed theatrical to the simple construction company director. "Glad to meet you!"

Don shook Luiz's hand somewhat reluctantly. Under this strange charismatic man's scrutiny, Don felt strangely naked and vulnerable, as if Luiz could see into his soul through those black, piercing eyes. Bella hadn't mentioned him in their previous conversation. Who was her to her? He had a mysterious air of danger about him.

One that Bella probably finds attractive, Don thought. He found himself suddenly feeling sick to his stomach. He knew he wasn't really ill, but he couldn't quite pinpoint his feelings. *What is that? Jealousy?*

"From what you've said about her, Romeo and Alison she would have got on well," Bella smiled at Don. "He's into the same kind of stuff… mysticism and magic."

"Uh-huh," Don said uneasily, trying to avoid Luiz's probing gaze. Don really didn't want to get into this.

"I don't just mean out of idle interest," Bella said quickly, misinterpreting Don's disinterest. "He is a scholar and qualified practitioner of the supernatural, too. A fully-fledged warlock and mystic…"

Instead of being reassured by this knowledge, Don positively recoiled, and Romeo Luiz took in this curious response, with interest.

"What's the matter?" asked Bella.

Don was saved from answering by the sudden ringing of the office telephone. He frowned in puzzlement, saying, "Sorry. It must be urgent. I asked my secretary not to put anyone through…" and reached for the phone.

After listening for a second, Don's face was stricken with shock. Romeo and Bella exchanged looks.

"Yes. OK. Put her through," he said, swallowing hard and turning his back on the group.

It was Jackie Nixon. "Darling! I've just heard that Belladonna Rose are in town!"

"Uh-huh," Don mumbled.

"And on your invitation? Is that right?"

Don cleared his throat. "Yes."

"Oh, I would utterly love to meet Bella Howard! She's one of my all-time favorite singers!"

"Really?"

"You must bring them over to meet me, Don."

"Oh, but…"

"You simply **MUST**!" she added threateningly, "Do you hear me, Don?"

Don swallowed again, and said quietly. "OK… I will. Sometime."

"Right away, Don," Jackie warned. "I simply cannot wait."

She put the phone down, leaving Don staring at the receiver, with his mouth open. He had no choice but to obey.

He turned to the band, three of whom had sat down and been chatting amongst themselves, while Bella and Romeo Luiz's eyes had bored into Don's back during his telephone conversation.

"Jackie Nixon wants to meet you." He relayed the fact in a dull tone. "Right now."

Bella's eyes gleamed, and her face lit up in excitement. "But that's fantastic! Romeo, you know I mentioned her to you!"

Romeo gave a self-satisfied smile, and narrowed his dark eyes. He knew. His intuition and psychic powers had already told him that this woman – this meeting would be significant. He just didn't know how. But clearly, it was fate that had brought them here, and fate that had driven this Jackie Nixon woman to get in touch now and invite them over. He was just delighted that this was playing out faster than he had anticipated.

"Let's go!" Bella said breezily. "Don, can you take us in your car? The crew can stay in the tour bus."

Don shrugged. "Sure. I'll bring you back, too."

No you won't, thought Romeo.

CHAPTER 11

"Of course, you must stay here!" Jackie gushed immediately, after greeting the band effusively in her dim hallway. "I insist! There are no decent hotels within easy distance of Melas, and you must be tired of being on the road."

She led the way into her living room, and the band members' eyes widened in amazement.

"Help yourselves!" Jackie waved an arm in the air, demonstrating that she had laid out in her living room all the accoutrements of a party any self-respecting rock stars could require.

"Fuck me!" gasped Cassie.

"Later, darl…" Ash murmured, as if in a trance. "I got work to do now!"

A table full of all manner of liquor, mixer drinks and glasses had magically appeared in the room since Don was last here. Another table at the side was laid out with small dishes of white powder, weed and resin, crystals, colored pills, small phials of liquid, and all the equipment necessary for any form of drug-taking – razor blades, small glass tiles, spoons, bongs, matches and lighters, cigarette papers, rubber tourniquets and hypodermic syringes.

"Jeez!" Lex Wild exclaimed, walking towards the table and running his fingers through a dish of brightly colored pills that clattered softly beneath his touch. "I'm like a kid in a candy store!"

Bella felt slightly sick. She had been hoping for a break from partying hard; for a change of scenery. Besides, she honestly wanted to be fully present during her time with Don. She wanted to savor the moments and recall the times of innocence she'd had, before everything in her life had gone crazy. She gazed across at the tables spread with goodies.

Maybe I'll just have one drink, she said to herself, her mouth watering.

Don had been very concerned that Jackie would zone in on him immediately, fixated as she was, but he need not have worried. As soon as Jackie had clapped eyes on Romeo Luiz, she was obsessed. Their eyes locked with great intensity, as if unspoken words were being passed between them. But done knew the look on Jackie's face meant one thing: lust. She had silently taken Romeo's hand and led him to one of the couches, where they now sat in deep conversation, Jackie clearly flirting with Romeo, and the mystical stranger clearly encouraging it.

Don couldn't help feeling greatly relieved: a burden had been taken from his shoulders.

Bella smiled at him gratefully. "Well, I was looking forward to talking to Jackie, but she seems to have been monopolized by Romeo," she laughed.

"Don't you mind her taking him away from you?" Don asked.

Bella looked at him oddly. "He's only a friend, Don!"

Romeo and Jackie were now kissing deeply on the couch. Romeo was lunging forward, practically on top of her, and Jackie's hands moved across his body in a frenzy. They were almost devouring one another.

Don laughed too, so pleased to be let off Jackie's hook. "Well, looks like you'll have to make do with my company."

"And that's no bad thing," she said, her laughing eyes staring into his, as she sipped her drink. "In fact, it's a very good thing."

Romeo and Jackie had instantly hit it off, both spiritually and romantically. It was as if they had known one another for centuries, the connection was so real and intense. They had only spent a few minutes talking – but talking deeply, finding a surprising commonality – before their urge for physicality had overtaken them.

Pushing him off her, Jackie gasped, "One moment."

Romeo sat back slightly in surprise as she stood up.

"Come," she said seductively, grabbing his hand and escorting him out of the room.

He followed her silently upstairs, eager for whatever might transpire. His mind had left his body – he was simply a throbbing physical machine of lust, driven by his body's needs. This woman had apparently cast a spell on him, and he didn't care to wonder. He just wanted to enjoy.

She closed the bedroom door behind them both and pushed him onto the bed.

"This time," she said aloud to herself. "I'm not going to waste an opportunity."

She unzipped Romeo's trousers, and his large erection popped out, released from its constraints.

Jackie's eyes gleamed with desire, and she slowly licked her lips. "My, my! What a big cock you have!"

"All the better to fuck you with," Romeo groaned, his voice thick with lust. He slipped his hand up her skirt, ripped down Jackie's skimpy panties and flung her onto her back.

"Wait," she said, pushing his arms aside, and getting onto her knees beside him, pulling her skirts up around her waist. She pinned his shoulders to the bed and straddled his straining member, slipping it inside her slickness, taking in its full length, in one slow lunge.

Romeo gasped in anticipation. His hips thrust upwards to meet hers, then back, and again, in increasingly faster movements, their pubic bones grinding and muscles engorging as they approached climax.

"Oh! Oh!" Romeo was completely mindless, his eyes rolled back in his head; lost in the moment; transfixed and transformed. He came at last, shuddering, in a loud guttural groan.

It was a full two seconds before he even realized that Jackie had bitten him hard on the neck. Two seconds before he felt the sharpness of the pain, and the pull of his blood as she sucked. And then, he was aware.

Jackie released Romeo's throat from the clamp of her jaws, and gazed down at his wide, frightened eyes. His own blood was on her lips, stained and smudged.

"Don't worry," she said, soothingly. "I'm not draining you. I'm just turning you."

"Turning me?" Romeo asked in a daze. He already felt different, as if a thrill of electricity was running through his veins. His skin was prickling with it, and he felt more alive than he ever had before.

"You're a warlock, aren't you?" she said, her eyes narrowed, analysing him. "I recognize your potential. We are like-minded, you and I, and it is only right that we are like-bodied. I need you, and others like you for what is to come. That's why I am giving you the greatest gift. The gift of immortality – I am turning you into a vampire."

From momentary fear and surprise, a slow grin of realization crept across Romeo Luiz's face. *What I could do with this power!*

She interpreted his sly grin correctly. "I knew you'd come round to my way of thinking, Romeo. Very easily."

"No thinking required," he winked, feeling a surge of excitement. "I am yours to command, Your Highness."

A smirk played on her lips. "Then, in that case, I have just the job for you…"

Cackling with conspiratorial laughter, the pair began plotting their great evil.

***

Meanwhile, downstairs, despite the music now playing loudly and the band partying, Don and Bella were in the process of rekindling their own romance. Both of them felt the need for some loving comfort. Bella's one drink had blossomed into three large ones, and Don himself was loosening up, too. They had kissed softly a few times, but it felt like their early courtship again, when they were teenagers, shy and chaste.

Bella was cautious, believing Alison to be still alive, and not wanting to upset Don's relationship, if he was happy.

"Are you happily married?" she asked him gently, hoping he would say that he wasn't. That he was open to a relationship with another person. With her.

He swallowed, considering his response. "I know she's dead, Bella."

"You *know*?" She had sat up in alarm, wondering how he could possibly know, unless he…

"I just know in my heart," he said sadly. "I know she wouldn't stay away. Wouldn't not contact me. Unless the worst had happened…"

Bella reached up to Don's face and rested her hand on his cheek, stroking his temple with her fingertips, trying to express her feelings of tenderness without words.

He went on: "I am as sure as I can possibly be, without evidence, that Alison is dead."

"But maybe, if you have hope…"

He shook his head emphatically, his grief-stricken eyes begging her to stop. "Don't, Bella."

"I'm so sorry, Don." She settled into his body, holding him close, even though they were surrounded by Cassie, Ash and Lex laughing, drinking and taking the drugs of their choice. Don and Bella were in their own bubble of intimacy.

Don had suspected that Alison had died long ago, so having it confirmed by Jackie had been almost a relief.

167

He'd had time to grieve a little and go some way to coming to terms, and although it hadn't exactly been enough time for him to move on with Bella, he certainly didn't feel he was being disrespectful towards Alison now she was dead.

I was disrespectful enough while she was alive, sleeping with Jackie... Anything I do now is nothing, compared with that.

Bella lay next to Don on the couch, one arm and one leg casually thrown over him, hugging him close. She was acutely aware of the heat of his thigh under the inside of hers. With her head on his shoulder, and his lips pressed to her forehead, this felt like home to her. He was running his hand through her hair, drawing out long blonde strands slowly between his fingers, then, when he got to the end, and released the lock, his hand would stray automatically back to her scalp and start again. It gave her thrills deeper than the last orgasm she's had.

This simple life, she said, wonderingly, to herself. *These simple pleasures.*

They had been chatting desultorily, despite the serious topics of their conversation. Don was telling her about what had happened to Mike – the shock of the huge bats, ripping out his throat.

"Like a vampire?" Bella said in surprise.

Don had shuddered, and lay in silence, brooding on the memory. Bella's mind was working, too, as she lay stroking her hand gently across Don's chest, deep in thought.

"I wish vampires were real," she said eventually.

"Yes, vampires are fucking real," Don replied bitterly. She felt his whole body go taut as steel, and tremble imperceptibly beneath her touch.

Her brow furrowed. "How can you say that?"

"Jackie Nixon is one," he said grimly.

"Yeah, right," Bella snorted in derision. "I know she was all over Romeo, sucking his face off, and maybe you don't like her, but – come *on!*"

He stayed rigid and silent, not knowing what to say. He'd already said too much. Maybe he should just let that one lie… or even disappear.

Of course, Bella was skeptical. She had no idea what was going on.

Don suddenly sat up, gently but firmly wrestling Bella's arm and leg off him.

"What's wrong?" Bella asked in surprise.

Don stood up, distracted, saying, "I've got to go."

"Have I done something?" Bella asked in concern. She got up, too, and followed Don across the room. She got a hold of Don's elbow for fear he should run off. "I thought we were getting on OK…"

As if he'd snapped out of a trance, he suddenly looked her full in the face and said genuinely, "Oh, Bella, we are. I'm so sorry. I just remembered something I have to do."

Bella allowed herself a reluctant pout. "Oh, I was so looking forward to spending time with you, Don…"

"I'm sorry. Tomorrow. I promise." He kissed her deeply on the lips. But although he allowed Bella to press her tongue into his mouth, longingly, he didn't reciprocate and she still had the impression he wasn't fully with her.

He left, and she felt desperately alone.

Get a grip, woman! she told herself. *It's not a rejection of me. The man's beloved wife is missing – presumed dead. He's hardly going to be in the mood for fucking an old girlfriend.*

Yet, she hoped, pouring herself another drink.

***

Back home, Don sat staring into space in the small pool of lamplight that pierced the darkness of his living room, nursing a bourbon on the rocks.

I should drink the whole bottle, he said. *Anesthetize myself. Kill myself, even. I wouldn't care.*

He put the glass to his lips and threw back his head, grimacing as he swallowed a large mouthful of the strong liquor. Normally, he only drank beer or at least if he had any spirits, he mixed his bourbon with Coke. But in the last week or two, his grocery shopping hadn't actually been a priority. Neat bourbon was all he had. He'd even run out of milk, and there was no bread, either.

Alison took care of that kind of thing, he thought sadly.

"But there's something you can take care of, for Alison!" a voice said.

He spun round in his chair, wild-eyed, clattering the glass down onto the coffee table.

There was no one there. He frowned. *Must have been my imagination.*

"No it wasn't…" said the voice.

This time, he sprang up on his feet, his heart pounding, ready to fight.

"Relax," the voice said. "It's only me!" And the ghost of Lucy Westerna materialized before his very eyes, developing like an old photograph from nothing at all, to a misty shadow, to the clearly distinguished figure of a young woman – just like a living human, although a little fuzzy at the edges, a little translucent.

Don's legs turned to water, and his knees crumpled, dropping him back into his chair.

"You should be used to me by now," she smiled, one ethereal eyebrow cocked in amusement.

"I'll never get used to… any of this," Don muttered, feeling foolish. Yes, he really shouldn't be surprised to see a ghost. After all, it had happened before, so he shouldn't be afraid. In fact, it was Lucy he had to thank for telling him the truth, so he felt he could trust her, no matter how crazy that sounded. He was just so jumpy, lately. Spending time in Jackie's company tonight, so on edge over the fact that she was a vampire, and that they had effectively killed Alison, had ripped his nerves to shreds.

"Why are you here?" he asked, recovering himself.

"In Alison's absence," Lucy said, "you are the only one who can help. You are in possession of the only thing that can defeat Jackie Nixon and her plan to initiate the great uprising of the sleeping vampires."

"What? What are you talking about?"

Lucy explained Jackie's intention to re-animate the Vampire City, and to awaken the thousands of vampires who were held immobile under an ancient spell.

"She intends to open the sleep-lock by performing a grave ritual," Lucy went on. "And if that devastation were not enough, all signs point to her unwittingly unleashing a force far worse than the vampire armies. One false move, and she could release upon the world the Red Beast of Hell!"

Don sat looking blank. "Sounds bad."

Lucy shook her head, laughing ironically. "You have no idea!"

"I just don't see how this concerns me," Don said. "Or how I could help... prevent this in any way..."

"You have the Grimoire Ţepeş!"

Don screwed up his face in incomprehension.

"It's a book!" Lucy cried in exasperation. "Did Alison never talk to you at all?"

Don shrugged. "Not about things I wouldn't understand."

"Man up!" shouted Lucy Westerna's ghost. "The future of the world relies on you!"

Don's eyebrows shot up in surprise. "That still doesn't motivate me. It just terrifies me."

Lucy's voice softened. "If it's any consolation, you are not alone. There are others who are on your side, who will help in the battle ahead. But you are actually within arms' reach of the answers. Therefore, you are the line of first defense. You only need look in a book that Alison brought to the house: the Grimoire Ţepeş." She spelled the title out for him. "It will show you exactly how to defeat the vampires."

Don shook his head. "But I've looked through Alison's papers and books already. I don't remember seeing anything with that name. I think I'd have remembered, because it's a weird title."

"Look harder!" Lucy insisted, and disappeared as suddenly as she had arrived.

Don took a gasp of breath. He stood up. Despite it being early morning and still pitch dark, he felt compelled to begin his search.

He walked through the house, suddenly filled with energy, despite the tiredness he had felt earlier. In the home office Alison had used, he looked first at the bookshelves, running his finger across the spines of the books, one by one, scouring the words for 'Grimoire Țepeș.'

He had scanned a third of the books, when his heart came up into his mouth. He saw the word: 'Grimoire' and gasped, snatching the book from the shelf in excitement and trepidation. But no. It was merely a book entitled 'Grimoires and Spellbooks.' He flicked it open. No sign of the word 'Țepeș,' but quickly speed-reading some content at least gave him an idea of the kind of book he was looking for. Seemingly, a 'grimoire' was a book of magic spells, owned by practitioners of witchcraft and other exponents of supernatural arts. Some of these books described how to make amulets and give protection. Others gave instructions and invocations to bring forth spirits and forces of good – or bad. He shuddered.

Placing the book back where he'd found it, he continued his search along the bookshelves. He found nothing like the book he was looking for. He sat back down at Alison's desk, surveying the piles he had looked through earlier. He flicked through them, for fear he had missed a book that might be concealed between the piles of loose leaves and cardboard envelope folders. He had no idea what the book would be like, so he reckoned he had better start again, in case he had missed it first time round.

He knew it was imperative that he did as Lucy had told him. He was prepared for doing some major searching and research amongst Alison's papers for the only book that would reveal ways to defeat vampires – and save the world.

CHAPTER 12

Will stood in the dark, outside the construction site, wondering exactly what to do next. He knew that within the site lay both Jackie Nixon's house – the old Madison place – and Alison Smith's home. One was a place of extreme danger; the other, of salvation.

He just had to figure out how to get into the Smith house to get his hands on the Grimoire Țepeș codex.

Checking in, now that he was so close, he communicated with Victor again, hoping that if he had some connection, Victor might give him some extra strength and power. At the very least, he might have some advice for him. Will still couldn't believe how helpful Victor was being, but he still recalled how genuinely terrified Victor had appeared when he mentioned that Jackie might inadvertently release the Red Beast of Hell. In spite of his past history, Will had to trust Victor: he had no other help, and he really wouldn't know what to do without him.

So, standing outside the fenced site of Melas under construction, Will mentally and spiritually called out to Victor: "Victor Rothenstein! I am here in Melas now. If the Grimoire Țepeș is definitely amongst Alison Smith's papers, I'm very close to laying my hands on it. Just now, I'm casing the construction camp, then I'll be working out how best to break into the Smiths' house to steal it."

Victor spoke back to him psychically: "Well, hurry up! Jackie now has fresh help…"

"Who?" Will interrupted.

"She has engaged a person called Romeo Luiz, who's a warlock possibly skillful enough to raise the sleeping vampire clan without incident."

"Shit. What do we do, then?"

"Our only hope now is another spell in the Grimoire, which will permanently seal the sleep-lock. It will render Jackie Nixon's powers useless."

Unknown to either of them, Jackie Nixon stood outside Victor's cell, her back leaning against the door and her eyes closed, silently hissing with fury. She had left Romeo Luiz in bed to recover from the exertions of his 'turning' – and also to keep an eye on the human revellers, while she had slipped down to the basement, through the portal and had flown into the Darkness to attend to matters within the vampire castle. Namely, preparing for the great ritual awakening – with Victor's aid, and checking on Kate's pregnancy.

To that end, she had just been approaching the heavy door of Victor's prison when she was brought to a standstill by a shocking psychic revelation. A voice in her head – speaking clearly and recognizably, as if talking in real life, to her face.

What she heard was: "… hurry up! Jackie now has fresh help…"

She recognized that voice – and suddenly became aware that she was listening in on Victor's thought processes. Was he talking to himself? In *her* head?

If she was close enough – a few yards from Victor while he was communicating with William via the vampire communication spell, Jackie, as Queen of the Vampires, was able to hear every word! This was a built-in design within the magic spell, to ensure that the Queen's closest advisors and entourage could not psychically talk to one another or plot against the Queen without her knowing. But Victor and Will were blissfully unaware of that fact, or her presence near to Victor. And this was also a shock to Jackie. She had stopped stock-still, her hand on the door, frozen.

There was a short pause. Then Victor continued: "She has engaged a person called Romeo Luiz, who's a warlock possibly skillful enough to raise the sleeping vampire clan without incident."

Jackie frowned. How did Victor know this? That was when she leant back against the door, pressing close, eavesdropping.

Victor had gone on, then, as if answering a question: "Our only hope now is another spell in the Grimoire, which will permanently seal the sleep-lock. It will render Jackie Nixon's powers useless."

The Grimoire? She knew that a grimoire was a book of spells… but what was this? *A grimoire that could make me powerless?* Were they… could they be talking about the legendary Grimoire Ţepeş? *Surely not!* It couldn't be! Her father had told her about this powerful spell-book, but he had never been able to get his hands on a copy. What did Victor mean by this? Jackie's face twisted in fury. *Obviously, treachery!* Victor was plotting against her! And who was Victor talking to? Working with? She seethed.

177

As if listening in to someone speaking on a telephone, she could only hear one side of the conversation. Clearly, there was another person involved, although she wasn't party to that person's responses. It was a psychic conversation she was happening upon, and she only had the power to listen to the vampire's thoughts – not the human's. And then, she was only able to do that during a vampire communication close to her – she could not read minds ordinarily, vampire or not.

Then she heard Victor say, psychically: "Fetch the book without delay, William!"

William? Jackie could barely suppress a hiss of horror. She was alarmed to hear that William was still alive at all – let alone that he was in cahoots with Victor. *Against me!* She could have roared with fury. And to hear about this book of spells, which would evidently be a major threat to her plans! She was incensed.

Her hands clawed, white-knuckled, and her fingernails were digging into the ancient wood of the door, as she struggled to take control and settle her breathing and her pounding heart.

Calm yourself! she thought. Her mind raced with thoughts and implications, quickly considering the best approach to take.

Ignorance! she concluded.

Once she had composed herself and Victor had been silent for several seconds, so she was sure that the vampire communication spell connection was broken for now, she swung open the prison door, and beamed at Victor.

"Victor, darling!" she cried, in a tone which was all sweetness and light. "The time is soon upon us. Tell me again, exactly, what we still need to do, to enact the ritual most precisely…"

Slightly rattled, having spoken to his co-conspirator just seconds before, therefore feeling guilty and self-conscious, Victor took a second to compose himself sufficiently to respond.

"Your Highness!" He bowed politely. "Of course! I would be delighted!"

He relayed the preparations still to be made and reiterated the procedures to be followed during the ritual, while Jackie paid lip-service to his instructions, all the while concealing her anger and outrage with a façade of calm coolness.

You sly, conniving bastard, she thought, whilst smiling indulgently. *You flatter me to my face, while you plot behind my back.*

"Thank you, Victor," she said charmingly, "You've been most helpful. You will be rewarded for all you have done, just as you deserve."

Once she had flounced off to check up on her sleeping daughter, Kate, in her own prison along the corridor, Victor was left to his own devices, to brood on recent events.

I've manged very well so far, he congratulated himself. *I think I've won Jackie round at last. And William still seems to trust me, too. Great result!*

He had been juggling the two parties to keep them onside. But little did he know that Jackie was now aware of his plans to defy her; although she had no knowledge of his true intent. William, meanwhile, was altogether

179

blissfully unaware of Victor's dissemblance. The human had no idea that the vampire was merely using him, and playing him for a fool.

Will still thinks I'm frightened of Jackie freeing the Red Beast of Hell, along with my fellow vampires! He actually allowed himself to chuckle aloud. *Poor human fool!*

Victor's major worry wasn't really that at all.

Once I have the Grimoire Ţepeş in my hands, I will have all I need!

What Victor Rothenstein was most afraid of was of Jackie Nixon becoming far too powerful. But she could be stopped – and when she was, Victor wanted that power for himself.

With the help of this most powerful codex, Victor's plan was to kill both William and Jackie. William would have served his purpose, and he would only get in the way of Victor's plans for himself. As an ex-priest and killer of vampires and demons, William was still a danger to Victor – more so if Will ever realized exactly what Victor had in mind.

Jackie was a dangerously arrogant woman – and a mere usurper of the power that should be Victor's. Victor hadn't lived for centuries – as the most powerful vampire to walk between worlds – only to have some newcomer take away his power – and what's more – take over all the greater power that could be unleashed! She was just some recently human woman! A fledgling vampire with no practical knowledge – only a self-serving megalomania and a bunch of tricks her human father had taught her!

But for the moment, up to this point, it had served him well to play along, to get her to pave the way for him to succeed when the time was ripe. She was merely a commis chef – a chopper and peeler and preparer of ingredients, for himself, the master chef to create a masterpiece! But he wouldn't merely create a dish of the gods. He would be the god! The all-powerful! The all-consuming!

Jackie has unwittingly prepared the way for me to take every advantage! he laughed to himself. *She does not realize how she serves me!*

Everything was lined up ready. Once he had removed Jackie and Will, using the power in Kate's unborn baby's blood, Victor would revive the vampire clan to serve himself. His eyes gleamed with excitement at the thought.

And then we will all feast on humanity!

***

After a short sleep, in which Romeo Luiz's body adjusted to the radical transformation he was going through, the now-vampire warlock woke up and strode downstairs, grinning.

"Hey, Ro," Bella drawled, trying to focus on him hazily, her hand swinging a glass of liquor in Romeo's direction, the amber liquid slopping over the side. Instead of sticking to one drink, or even three, she had lost count. And also smoked a few joints. She was pissed with Don for leaving, and although she was understanding of his emotional state and needs when she

181

was sober, she was now far from sober. She felt rejected, and deeply angry with him for rejecting her.

So when she saw Romeo coming downstairs, beaming and self-satisfied, she rounded on him. "Looks like you got yours!" she cried. "Cat got the cream... Pussy!"

Romeo smiled, not too widely. He was aware that his incisors had grown significantly, and he hadn't quite learned yet how to retract them in the company of humans. He felt quite thirsty for blood, but didn't want really to attack his friends. Unless it was absolutely necessary. His eyes scanned the tables laid out with drinks and drugs. If only there were some raw liver, or something that might stem his bloodlust... His eyes fell upon a bottle of ruby red... but it was merely red wine. He didn't feel that his system would be tricked by that for one second. But at the back of the table, behind the clusters of bottles of popular drinks: the whiskey, the vodka, the bourbon the tequila, he spotted an unlabeled bottle of a dark, rich almost dark-brown deeply red liquid. Romeo picked it up, and slightly tipped it over to one side. The liquid was thick and viscous, almost leaving clots at the side of the glass bottle, where the neck had been clear and transparent. His heart raced. He opened the bottle, his mouth watering, and the coppery metallic smell of human blood hit his senses. He almost laughed in delight, and placed his lips around the neck of the bottle, tipping back his chin and swallowing deeply.

AH! Such a relief! He almost gasped aloud. Jackie had thought of everything!

Instinctively, he knew it was nowhere near as good as fresh, new blood from a living human, but it served its purpose in staving off the craving. Temporarily, at least.

Draining the bottle, he wiped his mouth with the back of his hand, satisfied, and returned to the group, lounging on the sofas and chairs in a fog of weed-smoke, talking in a desultory manner. Except for Cassie, who had selected coke as her drug of choice. She was wide-eyed, animated, full of ideas and nervous energy. And coke.

Cassie was orating, "Yeah. She wouldn't mind, would she? She's like… Jackie's, like, man… cool! She'll be down with a party."

"Looks like you are partying already," smiled Romeo, self-consciously covering his growing incisors with his hand. Whilst he was certain that his best friend, Bella, would accept him as a vampire once he had explained what had happened to him and reassured her, he wasn't so sure about the rest of the band.

Sure, their Goth Metal Rock music is dark. Sure, their Goth culture embraces vampires and ghouls as cultural references. Sure, their clothing is reflective of all that… Romeo gazed around at them all, feeling strangely alien and apart. *Of course,* he realized, *I am a race apart.* They were entirely different beings from himself, now. Their music, their lifestyle, their culture all pointed to the fact that they would accept his vampirism. But he could not be certain, in reality.

They are wannabees. They are fantasists. What would they say if they knew? How would they react to the truth?

Would they be panicked and frightened? Stake him through the heart with the nearest implement? It was a risk he couldn't take, right now.

"It's-s-s-s-s..." said Bella, drawing out the final letter of the word as if she didn't know how to stop. She struggled to focus on Romeo's face, her eyes slightly glazed as his steady figure appeared to sway before her dancing eyes. "It's-s-s Lex's-s-s-s... birthday tomorrow..."

"And they wanna throw me a party," Lex Wilde said, nodding slowly and deeply several times with his eyes closed, as if lost in the music, just as he was when playing his keyboard with the band.

"Shshshshshsh!" Bella hissed at him, one finger held up against her lips. "'s a surprise!"

Lex doubled over with laughter, holding his sides. The rest of the band joined in, exaggerated roars of laughter providing a background for various hoots of: "Don't tell him!" and "Yeah! Surprise!"

Only Romeo was sober and serious, fully in control of himself. Except he hardly knew what 'himself' meant any more. He was wearing his vampire identity like a new, ill-fitting suit of clothing in a style he wasn't accustomed to – except it went far deeper than that – to his very core. He felt very odd, but he knew he would have to adjust to this new life. It was one of the laws of evolution. Adapt or die.

"Yeah!" Cassie gabbled on, her eyes bulging. "We wanna throw a surprise party for Lex. Here. Except so far, the only person who'll be surprised is Jackie!"

The band shouted and cackled. Everything was so funny. Everything was hilarious.

"Except it has to be – HUGE!" Bella asserted, opening her arms wide, her drink spilling out of the glass in her hand, splashing onto the leather seat of the couch.

"Cos Lex is so OLD!" cried Cassie.

"And WILD! Lex Wilde!" snickered Ash.

"Will she be OK with it, Ro?" Cassie asked urgently. "Jackie? Party girl?"

"Hostess with the moistest!" grinned Ash Abs, unaware of what he'd actually said.

"Moistest!" They all laughed uproariously.

Romeo looked around at them all, in their various states of inebriation, and said, steadily, "Oh, I am sure Jackie would be delighted to accommodate all your needs."

CHAPTER 13

In her daughter's prison bedroom, Jackie stood over Kate's constantly sleeping body, gazing at her pregnant form once again. A wry self-satisfied smile played on Jackie' lips, in spite of all that had gone on. She had called in to see her, as she did every day at some point, to survey the progress of her all-encompassing project. She was not innocently looking in on her spell-bound daughter and unborn grandchild: there was no sentimentality or concern attached to her interest whatsoever. Never having felt very maternal herself, to Jackie's sharp eyes, Kate was simply a vessel – a vehicle for a means to an end – and the girl's previously slim body now looked heavily bloated. Jackie congratulated herself on her power and success so far. She was delighted by how fast and well the baby was growing. The growth acceleration spell was working just as well as the sleeping spell had been doing – her magical powers seemed to be increasing, and the time was approaching when Jackie could reap the benefits of her skills and cunning.

Soon, she would be able to cut the squealing infant out of Kate's belly and sacrifice it, to achieve a greater good – for Jackie, at least. This unborn child's fresh blood and beating heart were the central elements of the ritual to give Jackie supreme power over the vampire underworld – and the human world, too, through her leadership of the undead troops. After all, what was a vampire queen without hordes of subjects eager to do her will? Under her direction, they would hold humanity in thrall. Jackie Nixon would effectively be both Queen of the Vampires and Empress of the Earth! Her time was so close – the significance so real, she could practically taste it. Jackie was almost vibrating with excitement, absolutely thrilled with the prospect.

But pestering her, lurking at the corners of her excitement, emerging from its place in the shadows, there was no doubt. Her imminent omnipotence was threatened by Victor's overheard revelation. The edge had been taken off her delight. Once again, her mind wandered back to the news she had recently discovered, and her brow furrowed, disgruntlement etched on her face.

She had seriously believed that she had eliminated all obstacles. But no. Victor's communication had completely destroyed that belief. Jackie's worry now was that William was still alive.

He has been incapacitated before, she reassured herself. *Next time, I will eradicate him myself, if that's what it takes. A puny human against the Queen of the Vampires? No competition.*

But what rankled her more was the fact that William was not alone in this. Victor was working with him.

Against me! she seethed. But the one thing she had over Victor was the fact that he had no idea that she was aware of his double-dealing and treachery. She would play that one close to her chest. She wasn't even sure

187

that she actually needed Victor and his arcane knowledge and vampire experience any more. She had learned enough – and now that she had the warlock and mystic, Romeo, on her side – did she need him at all?

But there was Don, too.

She had only recently made the connection. His wife was evidently the woman who had sprung out and attacked them that night, when the portal was opened – the woman whom Kate had killed. *And his wife, Alison Smith, had possessed a copy of the Grimoire Țepeș!*

She needed to act fast. Involuntarily, Jackie's hand strayed to Kate's swollen belly, where she idly laid it, contemplating her options.

Don had every reason to resent Jackie and want revenge. With this realization, Jackie was now aware that Don might do something very foolish and very damaging to Jackie's plan. Especially in the knowledge that Jackie was a vampire. Particularly if he had the codex by now.

As a mere human, Don was no threat to her at all. Safe in this knowledge, Jackie had only revealed to Don that she was a vampire to exert some power and sexual magnetism over him. But she had underestimated Don's investment in all this – the depth of his potential hatred of her, and his motivation to work against her.

His wife had the Grimoire Țepeș! Jackie hissed aloud at the very thought of it. Her father, Walter Pinkman had talked of this book – one of the most powerful books of spells in existence. Copies were rare, but they contained the very secrets of life – and undeath – itself. It contained spells which could control vampires – and even destroy them! If Don had laid his hands on it, driven by a need to avenge his mousy, studious wife – he could be a very dangerous man, indeed.

Jackie's enemies were close by. And they evidently posed more of a threat than she could have anticipated. But now that she knew the vultures were circling, she would be prepared.

She was jerked out of her reverie by a violent kick from the unborn baby that jolted her hand completely off her daughter's abdomen.

She laughed in surprise. *The time is coming – sooner than you think, child!*

***

Under Don's trembling fingers, the ancient printed diagrams danced before his disbelieving eyes. Just as Lucy Westerna's ghost had predicted, the Grimoire Țepeș had been in his house all along.

After scouring through the shelves, piles of papers and the desk drawers, in which he found the keys to Alison's small locked filing cabinet, Don had opened it and flicked through the suspension files inside. Eventually, reaching the last file at the back, he was shocked to see an old, leather-bound book. His heart beating fast, he drew it out, and read the gilded title embossed on the front: Grimoire Țepeș.

Much of the text was written in Latin, or at least, a language Don couldn't understand. Some words, he guessed. For example, 'diabolus' meant 'devil,' obviously giving rise to the word 'diabolical.' Just to demonstrate the point, there was an engraving of a devil with the word beneath it.

189

Carefully turning the fragile pages, Don had come across several pages with illustrations of vampires. The word 'lamia' seemed to feature a lot. Don wondered if this was the Latin word for vampire. The word 'succo' and 'suco' also appeared several times. *Is that like 'sucker'?*

Unable to make any progress in understanding the book, for safekeeping, he instinctively locked the Grimoire Ţepeş away in the filing cabinet again, wondering what his next step should be. He couldn't even figure out which one was the important spell, let alone understand exactly what he might need to do to stave off the danger Lucy Westerna had precisely warned him about.

If only Alison were there! He had considered this so many times during his grief after her disappearance, but he had never before longed for her ability to comprehend Latin! He needed someone who could translate this text – since it was beyond him. If only he had learned Latin at school…

But wait… hadn't Bella?

His heart leapt. Admittedly, Bella had gone off the rails academically and dropped out of school later on, but he knew she had taken Latin classes for a number of years, and she had always been sharp and intelligent. She would know way more than he did. The least she could do was tell him the gist of these spells and instructions; tell him which spell was the one he really needed to know, to keep the vampires at bay. Once he knew that, it would narrow it down and focus their attention. They could always check any exact meanings and unknown vocabulary on the internet if Bella's Latin

190

failed her. But at the moment, Don was overwhelmed and didn't know where to start. And he certainly didn't know who to ask. Apart from his old friend, Bella.

Looking doubtfully at his watch, he wondered if he could speak to her at this hour. It was still pitch dark outside, but time was of the essence.

He phoned her cellphone number, but nobody answered, and he cut off the call before her voicemail message started. He didn't want to speak to a machine. Maybe they were still partying. It looked like it was heading that way when he left. He felt a twinge of jealousy, wondering if she was sleeping with someone else tonight.

I need her.

He texted: CAN YOU COME OVER ASAP? I NEED YOUR HELP. DON.

To his surprise, the phone rang almost immediately after he sent it.

"Don? What is it?" Bella asked.

Don almost cried with relief, "Bella! It's hard to say over the phone – can you come straight away?"

"Sure…" Bella said, bewildered. "Give me your address… or some directions, at least. I'll be right over."

After he put the phone down, he paced the floor anxiously, fingering the tiny key of the filing cabinet like a protective talisman. He would explain everything to Bella first and ask her help, before showing her the Grimoire Țepeș that was locked in the cabinet.

Only minutes away, Bella soon burst through the front door he had left open for her.

Her face was stricken with concern. "What is it, Don?"

"Listen… this is going to be hard to believe…" he began, and swallowed down his emotion. "You'll think I'm crazy…"

She took his hand and listened, serious and silent, willing him to continue.

He cleared his throat. "You know… or maybe you don't… but… I have seen for myself that vampires do exist."

Bella gave a wry smile, which he interpreted as disbelief.

Don continued. "I have evidence, Bell… I've seen it with my own eyes…"

She stroked his hand reassuringly, whilst he told her all he knew about the bat creatures he had seen, with his own eyes, killing Mike Moran. Bella nodded her encouragement, so he felt able to reveal more of the story, clearing his head of all the confusion of thoughts and opinions that had been whirling chaotically around in his mind.

"And… as for Jackie… Oh, God…" He almost sobbed. "If you only knew…"

Bella squeezed his hand, keeping quiet. He glanced into her calm eyes, which held his gaze steadily while he struggled, weighing up whether or not he could trust her altogether. Deciding that he could. They had ancient history together, and he was gratified that their old intimacy had been renewed. And here she was, so kind and comforting now, that Don felt justified in disclosing to her Jackie Nixon's true nature as a vampire; what she'd told him about Alison's death; Lucy Westerna's ghostly visit, and what he'd discovered amongst Alison's

192

papers – "…the ancient Grimoire Țepeș that can defeat vampires."

He shrugged, his red-rimmed eyes searching hers. "Sorry to offload all of this on you, but… my intention is only to prove to you that vampires do exist."

"Oh," she smiled gently. "Don't worry. I know that they do."

"You do?" Don gasped with relief and almost laughed. It was so good to have an ally. He added, "I also want you to know what danger we're in, and how much I need your help with the translation of the spell."

"Which spell in particular?" she asked curiously.

"The one that will vanquish the vampires."

Bella laughed – a far too enthusiastic laugh. She tipped back her head and positively guffawed. Don's brow furrowed. There was something different about her suddenly, and he felt uneasy. She recovered herself, her suppressed giggles subsiding, and gazed at him.

"Oh, Don…" she said gently, amusement dancing in her eyes. "Why ever would I want to do that?"

Don's discomfort and wariness gradually turned to horror when, before his very eyes, Bella grinned widely, her lips peeled back to reveal sharp, elongated incisors.

"After all, I've just been turned into a vampire myself!" she hissed, a manic smile on her lips.

Don's face was frozen in a mask of shock and disbelief. "W…why?" Don stammered. "Why would you do that?" A million thoughts were spinning through his head. "Just explain why!"

"Stupid question," Bella replied with a smirk. "Jackie Nixon offered me eternal beauty and eternal youth. What woman in her right senses would turn that down?"

Her bandmates, Ash Abs and Lex Wilde, suddenly appeared in the doorway, grinning. They walked lithely across the room towards Bella and Don, their mouths and eyes mockingly wide. Both had the trademark red eyes and long fangs of the vampire race.

Don gasped at Bella. "You turned the rest of the band?"

Bella laughed. "Why not? You've gotta have friends!" She smiled at the drummer and keyboard player, "Get him boys!"

As the newly turned male vampires lunged for him, Don's instincts kicked in and his shocked paralysis was broken. He threw himself across the room towards an external wall's closed window and struggled with the window-lock, planning to leap out. His trembling fingers were useless in his panic.

"No such luck, darling," Bella chortled, as his ham-fisted attempts to open the window came to nothing.

He felt sharp fingers digging into his shoulders and arms, and he was flung bodily back into the center of the room with inhuman force. He landed heavily on his back, a sharp, intense pain suggesting that at least one of his ribs had broken. With his limbs sprawled out like a rag doll, he tried to use his remaining strength to get up, but Bella had already fallen upon him.

"Bella!" he cried in distress, attempting to wrestle against her attack both physically and emotionally. If there was some vestige of humanity left, maybe he could reach her.

It was not the petite, slim, lightweight human Bella that he knew, but a creature of monstrous power within Bella's body that had pinned him to the ground. He summoned up all his will to lash out with his one free arm, hoping to land a blow, but it was to no avail.

Screaming Bella's name and other indistinguishable cries, Don thrashed and fought for his life, but Bella had already sunk her fangs into his throat with some violence. As the searing pain registered in his neurology before Bella's powerful bite severed his spinal cord, Don gurgled in disbelief as he found himself paralyzed, his eyes bulging and his mouth stricken in a frozen rictus of shock and surprise. Before Bella could even pause in her first long, thirsty suck of hot blood, the rest of her vicious vampire band also fell upon his useless body, sinking their own fangs into his veins and arteries in a crazed blood-lust to take their fill before Bella took all the good stuff.

Blind and mad with hunger and thirst, Ash Abs and Lex Wilde joined Bella in their feeding frenzy, but hyped up by their collective madness, they tore Don limb from limb. Fortunately for him, Don quickly breathed his last. Having chewed and sucked at Don's right wrist, before wrenching the whole arm off in frustration, Ash sat slicing down the disembodied arm with one long fingernail, the frilly yellow fat exposing itself beneath the skin, as he licked and sucked at the remaining blood in the exposed veins, which dangled from his lips like spaghetti. After draining Donovan, Lex – as wild as his name – was really going to town on Don's abdomen, pulling out steaming, hot entrails with his teeth, having already ripped off one of Don's legs just for kicks and tossed it aside.

Bella raised her bloodied face from the shreds of Don's neck. Unused to drinking fresh blood from source, in her enthusiasm and drug-fueled rage, she had chewed through bone, muscle and cartilage, so that Don's head only remained attached to its torso by a thick flap of skin and flesh, where it had swung over his shoulder and onto the floor where he lay.

"Fuck," she muttered, looking down at her blood-stained clothing and spattered cleavage, whilst wiping her mouth with the back of her hand, simply smearing it further. "Hope these stains come out. This corset was my best!"

Roaring with laughter, Lex cried, "Let's teach him a lesson for ruining your outfit!"

The drugged-up male vampires, howling and cheering, tore Don's body to shreds in a flurry of teeth, fangs, nails and hands – the air momentarily thick with an explosion of shards of bloodied bone and lumps of flesh. Within seconds, the two had messily spread bits of Don's corpse across every surface. Lex had jumped straight onto Don's head with both heavy biker boots, smashing his skull into splinters and sending spongy brain matter everywhere.

"Hey! He's Mr Pumpkin head!" snickered Abs, observing the carnage.

Lex wiped a fleck of gray brain mush off the leg of his black jeans, and grinned. "You mean, he 'was'."

Bella, meanwhile, sat gazing in wonder at her bloodstained hands, like Lady MacBeth. On her palm sat the tiny filing cabinet key.

CHAPTER 14

William had spent some time orientating himself in the newly rebuilt Melas, to appraise himself of the potential dangers before he would finally break into Alison Smith's house to find the Grimoire. He needed to scope the area – determine his escape route, and alert himself to those around him.

To this end, Will had taken a walk around Melas, marveling at the changes since he had last been there – the town springing up anew at a remarkable pace. There still weren't many inhabitants at all, so much of the town lay in darkness, since the majority of the houses were still in a state of ongoing reconstruction. However, much of the external or structural work looked as if it was nearing completion. Presumably the internal work was in progress, too.

The sinister Madison House had been lit up like a Christmas tree – shadows flitting past the windows, and lights on both downstairs and upstairs. Either Jackie Nixon was here having a party, or a lot of people had broken into her home, too. He hoped that it was the former. This would offer him an advantage. If she was engaged in socializing at this time of night – or in fact, early hours of the morning – she would be no danger to him.

He had already identified Donovan Smith's dimly-lit home before checking out the rest of the town, and now returned to it, having established his plan and exit routes. But watching a couple of men enter the house, the lights and activity had suggested that there was something going on at there, too, so he had no choice but to lie in wait until people left.

Three people left, in the end, since a woman joined them – all of them squawking with laughter as they meandered off in the direction of the Madison House. More party-goers? In the darkness, he couldn't make out whether any one of them was Donovan Smith.

He waited uneasily for a couple of minutes, watching, but no lights went off, and no one appeared. There was no sign of movement. He glanced involuntarily at his watch. He couldn't afford to wait any longer, since he was already concerned that his reconnoiter had wasted some hours already. *I was foolish to be so cautious. I should have gone in earlier!* It was now or never. Maybe Donovan Smith had left with those others. Maybe he was already partying at the Madison House. Then again – maybe he was inside the house.

Better not take any chances, Will said to himself, stepping out of the deep shadows and making his way over to Donovan Smith's residence.

He tried the front door handle, and to his surprise, the door opened. *Unlocked?* He hadn't expected that.

A dim hall light on a small table was switched on, casting a small pool of yellow light in the penumbra. As soon as he stepped in through the doorway, Will felt a singular unease way beyond his fear of breaking into someone's house. There was a palpable sense of horror in the air that set all of Will's senses into overdrive. That, and the unmistakable tang of raw meat and faint metallic scent of blood that assailed his nostrils. As he crept forward into the light thrown by the table-lamp, beneath his feet, he noticed smudges on the polished wood flooring. He, reached for the lamp, and knelt down, tipping the hall light lower.

What the…?

A faint footprint. He dabbed his finger on it, peering close and sniffing. *In blood!* And more of them, tracking away from an open doorway ahead, towards the front door he had just entered.

Alert, he stood back up, and walked cautiously through the hallway, into the brighter living room.

He stopped dead in his tracks, his hand involuntarily covering his mouth, a gasp escaping. In the center of the room lay a small bundle of blood-soaked rags, but it appeared to be only the epicenter of a wide-ranging bloodbath. Or rather, there was not very much blood around at all, considering the blobs of minced meat, yellow fat and bone splinters scattered around the room. A large flap of skin hung down from a modest chandelier in the center of the room, where it attached piece of flesh was draped and beginning to cook near the lightbulb, just scenting the air with a smell reminiscent of pork.

What the fuck?

Will took a few wavering steps further in, in bewilderment, then stood taking in the horrific scene. Red fleshy lumps and papery skin were strewn across the couch, the floor, and stained the walls and even the ceiling. Appalled, but unable to stop himself, Will leant over the ragged bundle, and noticed that a collapsed Halloween mask lay beside it, one eye mushed, the other popped out like a table-tennis ball and hanging by a sinewy string. Brains spilt out of the crushed skull.

Except it's not a mask.

This had been a human, but Will had no idea what had happened here. The place was like a charnel house. Will had seen nothing like it since his battles with demons.

Hearing a sudden sound close behind him, Will swung around defensively, his foot slipping on a piece of gristle, causing him to slide onto the floor amongst the gore. Panicking, he rolled onto his side, and hitched himself up into a seated position, prepared for some kind of supernatural attack.

"Hands up!"

Will found himself staring down the barrel of a gun held by a uniformed police officer. Amazed, he held up his arms, open-mouthed.

"I… I can explain!" he stammered, knowing that he couldn't possibly. He spread his fingers wide. "I'm not armed."

The officer with the gun trained on Will stared fiercely at him, his teeth gritted. Another police officer – a woman – stared around the room in horror and disbelief. As her eyes scanned across the scene, her gaze reaching the crushed disembodied head of Donovan Smith spilling out its contents, she made audible gagging sounds before turning around and vomiting violently over her boots, the acrid scent of her regurgitated burger and stomach juices adding another layer to the fetidness of the atmosphere.

"Contaminating the scene," muttered the gunman.

The female police officer wiped her sweating brow with her sleeve and turned around. "Fuck you." She addressed Will. "Name?"

"William McConnellson III," Will breathed, relieved that it was only the police he was dealing with, rather than anything worse.

"William McConnellson III," repeated the woman officer, "I am arresting you on suspicion of murder."

"What?" Will gasped, incredulous.

"You have the right…"

"Wait! Wait!" Will interrupted, his eyes wild. *I have to find the Grimoire, for fucksake!*

The female officer continued, "…to remain silent and refuse to answer questions."

"Listen! I've got to find a book…"

"Anything you do say may be used against you in a court of law…"

While the female officer recited the Miranda, the male kept looking straight down the barrel of the gun at Will, the safety catch off. The man's top lip sneered, his eyes fixed on Will, furious. His trigger finger twitched.

Will visibly deflated, all power gone. Rambling about vampires and demons and spells was not going to help his case; he could tell.

*　*　*

Victor, still in chains in the Darkness, was desperately trying to connect with William. Jackie had left the castle, which had given Victor time to warn his human ally that she was on her way back to Melas, but for some reason, the vampire communication spell didn't seem to be working. And that concerned him.

Time was relatively meaningless in the Darkness, but he estimated that hours had gone by since William had told him he was in Melas, ready to break into the Smiths' house, where the Grimoire Țepeș was – they both hoped. He should have achieved it by now. So why couldn't Victor hear him?

Victor couldn't understand why the communication spell wasn't working. He understood that if Will's mind was firmly concentrating on other things, or if under stress – the connection might not work – just like a telephone line that was busy while the person was already engaged in another call. But for so long?

Had something gone wrong?

Victor wracked his brain for any kind of explanation that might reassure him that William wasn't dead.

Not that he cared whether William was dead or not. But Victor needed that book.

***

Jackie smiled in satisfaction, and raised a glass to Lex, who winked at her lasciviously as he passed by the couch where she lay lounging with her feet up like the Queen of Sheba.

Instead of Queen of the Vampires! I am almost Empress of the Earth and the Underworld!

Almost crazed with power, she could hardly contain her delight! One anonymous call to the police from a 'concerned citizen', claiming she was suspicious of a man wandering around Melas, lurking in the shadows and spying on people, was all it had taken. It was almost ridiculous to think that the Queen of the Vampires had got rid of her mortal enemy with one phone call to the human police!

She laughed aloud at the thought, completely tickled by the situation.

All Jackie had wanted was for the police to take Will in for questioning for a few hours, keeping him out of the way while she prepared for the ritual. But the timing could not have been more perfect if she had planned it! For the police to apprehend Will at the very moment that he had blood on his hands – literally – was joyously ironic. Talk about being 'caught red-handed'! Now he would be detained for a matter of days, at least – even if he was found innocent – rather than hours. By the time he was let loose, it would be too late for him to interfere.

In one fell swoop – simply by 'turning' Bella and the band, and sending them over to Don's house – Jackie had skillfully eliminated the threat of both Donovan and William within minutes of one another. Bella and the boys had brought her the Grimoire Țepeș – which she could hardly prevent herself from poring over immediately. But she could luxuriate in the knowledge that there was plenty of time for that later. With Romeo Luiz's knowledge, experience and mystical powers, she already felt invincible. Having the Grimoire Țepeș was just the icing on the cake. The main thing was that it was in *her* hands – no one else's.

And while Victor was still incarcerated in the castle, although she might not require his services any longer, she had nothing to fear from him, either. She would deal with him later.

But for now, she had bought herself more time, and she would use that time to celebrate!

Yes, they would throw a party for Lex Wilde's birthday. And yes – it would all suit Jackie's devilish plan.

"We have lots to do," she announced to her bedraggled guests, who had been partying hard for hours. *In fact, I have so much to do, I can't afford to visit the Darkness – until later.*

"I can do without sleep. But you newbies may need some time to adjust. I suggest you replenish your energy by getting some sleep in my guest rooms. You will be quite safe here. Daylight does not penetrate the window panes, and there are heavy drapes in the bedrooms."

Bella had to confess, she was exhausted. "Sounds like a great idea. We have another heavy night ahead. You notified everyone, Lex?"

"Uh-huh," Lex affirmed, glancing at his cellphone. Another confirmation by text. "This is gonna be RAD!"

As soon as Jackie had agreed to host the party, just as the others had guessed she would, there had been a flurry of social media, text and phone messages. To be honest, Lex had started inviting people as soon as the idea was mooted between the band members. He didn't even bother asking Jackie before he started the chains and networks of communication alight. He had figured on her being too polite to say no if a celebrity turned up on her doorstep to wish her house-guest a happy birthday.

What's she gonna do? Turn them away? was his logic.

So, already, plane flights were booked – and some of Lex's wide circle of friends and associates were already winging their way to Melas.

"OK, so…" Lex paused on his way out of the room and gestured with one hand, as if trying to summon up the right words. "Good night. Or… good day!"

Romeo stepped close to Jackie, looking down on her flirtatiously. He raised a quizzical eyebrow. "Sure you're not coming to bed?"

She laughed, and patted his chest. "You need to conserve your energy, too, darling. We have a great mission to fulfill. Go get some rest."

With Jackie fully on board with the party, after daylight broke and the shades were drawn thicker, her staff team arrived, and she set them to work straight away. Jackie engaged her PAs and house staff in booking stage blocks and refreshments, and decorating her home in preparation for a huge celebrity party that night. The guest list for Lex's birthday party read like a who's who of rockers and film stars. An important person in her own, earthly right, Jackie had her own A-list of invitees, herself. And also, some hangers-on and wannabes who would be completely necessary for her illicit purposes.

With the new vampires all tucked up in bed in the dark, and preparations well under way for the party – facilitated by her team of staff, Jackie now had the luxury of time alone to spend with the Grimoire Țepeș. She wanted to learn all she could about the process she was about to initiate. Even though Romeo Luiz was

205

completely capable of undertaking the ritual for her, Jackie didn't like to depend on too many people. She had only known Romeo for a matter of hours, and although she implicitly trusted him – her trust was limited. She was naturally suspicious, and wanted to be in control of every situation that was important to her. The only person she could truly trust was herself. Therefore, the more she knew, the better.

In the quietude of her home office, behind a locked door so that her bustling staff definitely could not disturb her, Jackie opened the ancient, leather cover of the tome. She held her breath, wondering at the words on the faded parchment of the pages.

She read, hungrily, eager to consume all of it at once. Her heart was beating fast, adrenaline pumping. *This is better than sex!* She wanted to simultaneously flick through the whole book fast to know what it contained as a complete work, and yet, she wanted to linger and absorb it completely – to pore over every word, every detail. She was greedy for it all.

Her father, Walter Pinkman, had trained her well, obsessed as he had been his whole life with studying magic and later, after she had left for college, he had devoted himself to serving the vampire Victor Rothenstein, and garnering more information on supernatural matters. As a single parent, when Jackie was tiny, he hadn't allowed a small daughter to get in the way of his thirst for knowledge – instead, he had drawn her into helping him with his research, and she had kept up that interest even after she left home. Since an understanding of classical languages like Aramaic were essential to the gathering of such knowledge,

Jackie's Latin was impeccable, so she perfectly comprehended every word in the Grimoire. After a lifetime of studying magic, symbols and other arcane knowledge, her recognition of specific demons by name and by the sight of their illustrations meant that she very swiftly identified the specific spell that would open the sleep-lock and enable the vampire hordes to rise from their slumber and obey her command. But there was so much more! She spent the whole day lavishing attention on every spell in the book, drinking it in and committing it to memory. To an ambitious and powerful vampire such as Jackie Nixon, this was a treasure trove. This was the Holy Grail. This was the means to everything she wanted.

***

Lying on his back on the wafer-thin mattress in the police holding cell after hours of interrogation, Will stared fixedly at the ceiling.

His mind was restless, and he was physically and mentally exhausted, but he knew that he needed to communicate with Victor now. He had been ignoring Victor's urgent callings – his mind reaching out to him. Will had grown to dread the sensation of pure evil emanating from Victor each time they communicated telepathically – no matter how far away he was. That evil feeling was so insistent and pervasive that it seemed to consume Will himself – filling him with a terrifying wickedness, and this evil apparently increased with each occasion they had used the spell. Will had put it off up to this point. Besides, everything had been too frenzied up to now – Will had been attacked, been arrested, been questioned – he had not had a moment to think, and he needed to clear his mind as far as he could, to be receptive to the vibrations of Victor's thoughts, too. So, swallowing down the bile that had risen in his throat, Will reached out with his mind.

"Where the hell have you been?" came Victor's thoughts, urgent and angry. Already, a gradually developing wave of pure evil was lapping at the shores of Will's mind.

"Don't ask," Will answered. "Suffice to say, I do *not* have the Grimoire Țepeș…"

"What?" came a roar in Will's head, and a sickening flow of nausea consumed him. "Then get it! Now!"

"I can't. I'm locked up in a police cell."

There was a silence in Will's mind, but the putrid feeling of Victor's wickedness increased, making Will feel dizzy.

Then: "You fool!" Victor roared. "Where is the book?"

"I… don't know," Will admitted, "but I suspect someone else has taken it…"

A hugely loud roar from Victor rattled Will's head, making him wince with the pain of it.

CHAPTER 15

Romeo Luiz stood with his hands in his pockets, casually leaning against the wall, a sneer creeping across his lips. Lex Wilde's birthday party was in full swing, the air hot with the sweat of pressing bodies; the constant chatter of people and squawks of self-promoting laughter almost drowning out the rock music from the temporary stage in Jackie Nixon's back yard where the first act, Abra Cadaver, was playing. They had toned down their stage set for the more modest venue. Jackie's house was a mansion, but certainly not as capacious as the arenas they usually played, so they had set up and played outside, and people moved in and out of the wide double French doors, fetching cocktails and other drinks, eating snacks and generally making sure of having seen and been seen by the publicists, other celebrities, and their entourages.

Romeo watched the people come and go, moving from one room to the other; inside to outside. A few individuals had already disappeared completely. He smiled to himself, and nodded. This was all going to plan. He could feel the energy rising, and it was almost at the optimum level.

Even the relatively modest back yard was full, once the stage had been set up, and groups of chairs and tables set out. Space on the lawn in front of the stage allowed for a mosh pit should people wish to really get into the music, but to most of the assembled crowd, the band was merely background to their own entertainment, as recreational drugs were taken, booze drunk, bitching progressed, gossip was made and deals were done. But the crowds and the distractions were all to serve one purpose, and one purpose alone. And it had nothing to do with celebrating Lex Wilde's birthday.

Ash Abs' reptilian eyes darted around shiftily, before he leant in to one of the groupies, a buxom brunette called Sara, who had come along with Abra Cadaver. He muttered to her, his breath hot and moist on her ear: "Join me in the second bedroom on the left, in two minutes' time."

Wow! she thought. *I was hoping to get with Luther, the drummer with Abra Cadaver again. But – hey! Ash Abs! THE Ash Abs from Belladonna Rose!*

She couldn't believe her luck. The dark-haired woman gazed into his eyes, grinned lasciviously and nodded.

Ash turned and stealthily wound his way between conversing people, then he sprinted upstairs, pushing past others who were seated on the staircase or wandering down from the upstairs bathroom because the downstairs one was in use. Sara waited a minute, then stood up somewhat unsteadily, tugged down her corset belt and adjusted the white silk blouse at her cleavage before she sashayed towards the staircase, a sly smile on her face, following in Ash's footsteps towards the second bedroom on the left.

As she picked her way up the stairs, stepping around the party-goers lounging on the steps, they were too self-absorbed to notice that only half the people who went upstairs actually came back down again.

On the landing above them, Sara, the dark haired groupie, ran her black-nail-polished talons through her hair, fluffing it up, before she spread her fingers against the door to the second bedroom on the left and pushed it open. She bit her lower lip coyly, preparing for the best sex of her life. Frankly, it didn't matter what the sex was like – just the fact that it was with Ash Abs was enough for her. Another one for the collection, although each time she offered herself up, she secretly hoped she would be the one to win the heart of the next up-and-coming musician she slept with. The one to reap the benefit from fame, wealth and good fortune. She lived in hope.

But not for long.

Stepping into the dimly-lit room – *how romantic!* – she closed the door behind her, eagerly squinting in the half dark to see if Abs was already in bed. A flurry of movement from behind the door in her peripheral vision caught her attention, and she felt the weight of a quick scything blow to her neck, and found that the front of her blouse was suddenly wet from a cloud of gushing liquid apparently from nowhere.

What the hell? she tried to exclaim, her eyes bulging in surprise. But no sound came out. Her mouth worked open and closed uselessly, but she was unable even to cry out, as her legs slowly gave way, crumpling beneath her. She lifted her hands to her throat, feeling a wet fleshiness under her fingertips, drenched by a fairly hot liquid. She blinked in incomprehension, gazing at her hands and saw a pool of dark blood on them, dripping through her fingers.

What? she wondered in amazement as the floor hit her face. *It didn't even hurt,* she said to herself as she died.

Ash stood over her, the knife in his hands. He even switched on the main ceiling light, because this was amazing to see.

"Fucking shame to waste it," he muttered aloud, watching the blood that had pumped from her sliced throat now simply trickle and pool on the polished hardwood floor.

But that's what he and the others had been told, by Romeo and Jackie. *No drinking the blood, this time. Let it flow.*

"Let it flow, let it flow, let it flow!" sang Abs wryly, to the Christmas tune, *Let It Snow*. Never had such a happy song sounded so sinister.

He licked the blade of the dripping knife, both sides, while he stared at the thick red puddle of blood with longing, his mouth watering. But despite himself – this next part was the best bit. Tonight, he'd done this five times now, and he never tired of it. Still could barely believe his eyes.

The puddle of crimson blood was so perfect that it even had a meniscus – a wobbling dome like a 'skin' of surface tension that held its shape. It was shrinking – but not getting smaller as you might expect from a liquid that was draining away. The floorboards were sucking in the blood directly, so instead of the width of the puddle narrowing, the depth of the blood became shallower as the blood was sinking down straight into the wood. But what was even more remarkable was the fact that within seconds, all of the blood was gone. The timber was perfectly clean, as normal. No stains, no signs of bloodshed. And then, more remarkably still, the dead body lying on the floor began to be absorbed into the floor, too. Ash could hear a faint sucking sound, above the thrum of the music outside. As if Sara's body was slowly sinking beneath the surface of an expanse of water, she disappeared downwards, being absorbed into the structure of the house. Ash stood staring, fascinated. Last to go was a tangle of her dark brown hair, which swirled around like pondweed in a final slow rotation as if a plug had been taken out of a sink. All that remained was drawn down by some infernal suction until there was nothing left but the highly-polished, recently fitted expensive timber floorboards.

With a nod of satisfaction, Ash left the room, in search of his next victim.

***

Downstairs, Romeo closed his eyes for a moment, the thrumming of a pulse within the house was getting louder to his inner ears. *Soon. Very soon.*

The rest of the band had been busy all night. While everyone was having fun at the party, the vampires had taken the opportunity to fulfil the needs of Jackie Nixon in a most peculiar way, and had begun murdering selected groupies, hangers-on, and hookers; mostly people no one would miss. Once they were dead, their bodies and blood were absorbed into the Madison House's floor.

Lex Wilde – the birthday boy – had been most visible downstairs – as guest of honor, he needed to be seen, since people expected to wish him well, present gifts, fetch him drinks and fawn over him. But that hadn't stopped him doing his share to fulfil their new purpose. He had killed a couple himself, although he could barely afford the time to watch the incredible process of absorption, since there was forever someone calling out his name, wanting to give him give him birthday greetings and presents. Bella, too, was pulling her own weight in the death toll, and voracious in her attention to detail.

In bedroom number one, the master suite, their band member, Cassie Dean, was biting a chunk of neck out of a guy she had also enticed upstairs. The feel of her teeth initially excited the guy, thrillingly pressing into his throat while one of his hands squeezed her breast and the other clamped onto her ass. But then his lust turned to pain and horror as her teeth went all the way, biting through skin, flesh and further still, into veins and arteries, eventually meeting together, her canines and incisors having worked their way through the gristle of his torn throat. Cassie kept her mouth over the wound momentarily, stemming the gush of blood while his eyes widened in shock, and his bony fingers dug into her upper arms. She at last stepped away from the arterial spray, reluctantly allowing the warm blood she had trapped in her mouth to drip out of her open lips onto the thirsty floor. The guy clapped his hands over his neck, trying to stop the flow – the gurgling sounds in his throat amusing Cassie almost as much as the incredulous, helpless look on his face. He staggered one step towards the bed, then fell onto his knees with a hard crack, before rolling onto his side as the last of the blood, without a beating heart to pump it any longer, slowly dripped out. The floor was already drinking it in.

Cassie stood with her hands on her hips, watching the remarkable process at her feet, chewing the chunk of flesh she still had in her mouth like a piece of gum. She was champing down, over and over, rolling it around her mouth, sucking as much of the juice out of it as she could, although it wasn't very muscular – mostly skin and some sinewy blood vessels. *Can I just eat this one piece?* she wondered. *Will it matter?*

She soon had it reduced down to a piece of dry felt. Guiltily, she spat it on the ground. *Just in case.* It was gone within a second, absorbed into the fabric of the floor.

Cassie brushed a lock of red curly hair from her eyes with the back of her hand, then noticed the blood on her fingers. She licked it off, like an animal cleaning its fur.

***

Time was moving on. The energy was increasing with every moment – even Bella could feel it. This burgeoning power was added to that of the hundreds of soul stones Jackie had insisted were concreted into the foundations of the building – the essence of human souls was literally embodied in the structure of the Madison house. The incredible energy of the portal was almost at bursting point, and in response to some vestigial connection, Bella's very bones ached with a yearning for some kind of release. *The time must be imminent.*

Across the crowded living room, Bella met Romeo's eyes and gave him a questioning look. Romeo nodded darkly, and moved fluidly out into the hallway, brushing past the laughing, drinking guests. Bella followed him down the corridor towards the basement door.

"Stay here," he told her.

"Have we done enough?" she asked urgently. "Will it work?"

"Yes," he answered, one tanned hand on the doorknob. "Your work is done. The rest is up to us."

Then he left her surrounded by the life and soul of the party and stepped inside the entrance to the dark. Closing the door behind him, he slid a heavy bolt across it before he walked down the staircase and into the expanse of the cellar itself.

Down below, an immersive, dim red light emanated from nowhere and reached everywhere. The walls seemed to glow with a yellow translucence, solid red veins and arteries threading from floor to ceiling which throbbed with the steady rhythm of a heartbeat, as if pulsating with life. They were encapsulated inside a living, breathing thing.

Victor sat on the floor in one dark corner, bound in chains, scowling beneath his brows. He had been attempting to communicate with William for the past hour, to no avail. Either William was dead, or blocking him in some way. Dejected, Victor admitted defeat and slumped, powerlessly looking on. His fate lay in Jackie Nixon's hands. As did the fate of humankind.

Jackie Nixon, dressed in a long ceremonial red robe, stood in the center of the cellar, a manic grin on her face. She could barely contain her excitement. Held tightly in her arms and pressed against her chest was the Grimoire Țepeș.

"And you're sure we no longer need the baby's blood?" she asked Romeo, as if mid-conversation. "For the ritual to work properly?"

"No," Romeo answered, smiling. "You have me – which is enough in itself…"

"Oh, ho! Such arrogance!" Jackie sneered, her eyebrows arched.

"… and you have the Grimoire Țepeș, moreover," Romeo continued, staring at the book in her hands. "We have sufficient energy from all those killed tonight to flood the Soul House with blood, bodies and souls. All of this is power enough. Can you not feel it? To take your daughter's baby's blood would be overkill."

"I love overkill," Jackie said, pouting for effect, although her wicked eyes held laughter. "I love any kind of kill."

"Sufficient blood has been spilt. We do not need the newborn blood sacrifice. We have all we need here to reopen the vampire sleep-lock without that," he assured her.

"What a shame. What a waste. Perhaps we can use the infant for something else." Jackie added airily, "Otherwise, we may as well kill it now."

"There is another ritual we might use later, once the sleep-lock is opened," Romeo interjected. "The child, once born, can be used for the ritual to increase the power of the vampire armies, permitting the vampires to take over the world – and enabling you to take over both that and the underworld, too. That requires the blood of an innocent."

Jackie clapped her hands together in delight. "Make it so!"

"But first, this. Your daughter may sleep on for a while."

"We must find a use for Victor, too – my treacherous servant. Simple killing is too good for him." At this remark, Victor gave a low hiss.

"Perhaps," Romeo said dismissively. "But we must first move on to the main event – the release ritual. While the time is ripe."

"Any riper, it would be like a rotting fruit," Jackie said, handing Romeo the Grimoire Țepeș.

She strode across to the altar – a long, waist-high stone block draped in a black cloth – she had set up before the cellar wall that gave onto the Darkness itself. A bleached goat's skull stood on the black silk in the center of a painted pentagram: a sparkling silver circle with a gold pentangle inside it. She held one hand up in the air, her outstretched fingers directed at the wall, as she had done every day since she first opened the portal to move between the worlds. A dark hole opened up instantaneously, gaping widely like the snarling maw of a hell-hound.

"Get on with it, Luiz," she commanded.

Romeo bridled slightly at her tone. *Who does she think I am? To speak to me like that! Nevertheless,* he answered his own question, *undeniably, she is my mistress.* He obeyed and stepped forward, opening up the Grimoire Țepeș at the relevant page.

Jackie knelt down in front of the altar, her crimson robes billowing out and rippling like a waterfall of blood. She raised her arms in the air, and Romeo took this as his cue to start the incantation.

"Lamia! Omni!" Romeo commenced addressing the sleeping vampires.

The house appeared to hold its breath. The pungent scent of blood was heavy in the air.

***

Will had the taste of blood in his mouth. He swallowed hard, rubbing his tongue on the back of his teeth. But there it was, still. The metallic tang. Unaccountable. In the police cell, he held onto the bars with his white knuckles and pressed his face against them again. One more try.

"Officers!" he yelled again. But they had long ago stopped listening to his crazy talk. They didn't even acknowledge his cries for help. As far as they were concerned, if he was yelling, he was still alive. That was a bonus when people die in custody every day. Besides, he was a lunatic, rambling about vampires and the devil and the end of the world. An everyday crazy. Let him cry himself out, then sleep off whatever drugs he'd taken. Or, they could call the psych people in the morning. Let him be their problem.

Will continued, "Please! Listen to me!"

He had heard nothing from Victor for hours, had even tried his hardest to communicate, despite his hatred of connection – but nothing. It was as if the spell was broken. Was Victor even still alive? And yet, in his guts,

Will could sense the growing evil. What was happening?

***

Romeo continued orating, his voice grave and stentorious: *"Phasmatos Salves Nas Ex Malon, Terra Mora Vantis Quo Incandis, Et Vasa Quo Ero Signos!"*

The walls palpably began to pulsate. Jackie's eyes gleamed, her excitement increasing, her teeth bared in a rictus grin.

Victor braced himself. He could only guess what was coming.

***

Belladonna Rose rocked on in the Madison House, fueled by the thrill of the energy rising within the building, spreading out into the backyard, and connecting down into the Darkness – and beyond. For their drug and drink-addled audience, the soul-shaking vibrations beneath their feet were just proof of the power of the band's heavy rock music – and the high quality and volume of the amps. The throb of the bassline hit them right in the heart, syncopating the rhythm of their bodies with the music and unknown to them – the pulse of the house itself, fed by blood, flesh, bone and souls.

A mass of sweating bodies writhed and swayed and jumped and yelled. Belladonna Rose were whipping up a frenzy, and the energy of their listening crowd fed the band's own thrilling sense of what was to come. The beat went on. The excitement increased.

***

"Singuinata Venet a Superem!" Romeo gently tipped a pewter goblet over the goat's skull, spilling thickening blood which coated the shockingly white bone surface with an equally horrifying rich red frosting.

Jackie's breathing rate increased. She panted, grinning widely, staring hypnotically into the depths of the cavernous portal, waiting expectantly. Tiny gasps of ecstasy escaped her lips, as she felt the intensity of the call – the primal, multi-sensory connection with the slow stirring of a legion of vampire bodies from the crypts and graves and mausoleums surrounding and beneath the Vampire Castle. Deep in her cold vampire heart, she sensed the gradual awakening of the ancients of her tribe.

She felt the calling, too, and she rose to her feet and stepped forward into the thick of the Darkness. She would fly. She could not wait to greet her legionaries, and she wished to meet them there in the expanse of their own realm, not in some cramped basement of human design.

The sleep-lock was opening, and she could intuitively feel the imminent surge into life of a thousand vampires. And that was just the beginning.

In his corner of the basement, Victor sat in chains, enraged by the audacity of Jackie Nixon, but also deeply horrified by what he saw and he felt, too. He was connected by this innate, urgent, throbbing pull towards his undead countrymen, but he also knew what this meant. And it shook him to the core. Jackie Nixon was a power-crazed megalomaniac who had no idea – no experience – no awareness at all of what she was unleashing. She and Romeo Luiz simply did not know what they had done. To his dismay, Romeo's summoning spell appeared to be working, and worse still, they had fed the Soul House way beyond its basic need. With every fresh drop of blood, the house's living malevolence was increasing, and yet these two recently-human upstarts had no awareness of the meaning of this fact, nor of the horrifying implications. Not only was the house now alive with evil, but Jackie Nixon was out of control, the vampires were marching, and the Red Beast was in danger of being released – all of which would spell the apocalypse. Victor was terrified for the first time in all his centuries of being undead.

"Medareno sometswar! Medareno sometswar!" cried Romeo Luiz in delight.

He lowered his hands, satisfied. "It is done."

***

In the Darkness, the curse was broken. The atmosphere was thick with anticipation and the malevolence that had always hung brooding in the air was sharp and threatening, like a weapon. If Jackie stopped to consider this, even she would feel the danger to herself. But her excitement was too great. She didn't stop. She didn't think.

Jackie stood regally dressed in her ceremonial robes, smiling ecstatically as she surveyed her troops moving towards her. As far as the eye could see in the purplish glow of the Vampire lands within the Darkness, there were thousands of solitary figures approaching. They walked with a variety of gaits indicative of their personalities and condition: some striding out, some stumbling; some stepping stiffly or tentatively, having lain immobile for several centuries. But together they made a shifting, live, undead blanket clothing the landscape. The sleeping vampires had all awakened and as they gathered near, they bowed before Jackie.

Jackie's eyes gleamed with madness.

***

Above, in the earthly realm, Belladonna Rose were reaching the climax of their impromptu show in the backyard of the Madison House. They too, could feel the upsurge of thrilling power that called their kind back to life in the Darkness. The thrill of killing – the house's living, breathing presence – the ritual – the vampires' awakening – all contributed to this spectacular finale.

The house pulsated and brooded.

Sweating and fixated on sublimating and channeling their unnatural urges into their music, the band cast feverish gazes at one another as they played, whipping their celebrity guest audience into a trance of doomed delirium with their clashing metallic sound and booming bass. Sailing out over it all, singing of exquisite pain and death, was Bella's voice, in turns hauntingly melancholic or operatically screaming, loud and strong, striking at the hearts of the partygoers. Speaking to them deeply. Lex's hands were running up and down the keyboard, improvising music never heard before. Abs' drums pounded to the beating hearts of the party – to the heart of the house itself – then led into a spectacular explosion of sound that left the audience gasping and amazed. Belladonna Rose had never sounded so good; so impassioned; so unreal. And their audience knew it – driven wild by the spectacular rhythm and surprised by the overall power and harmonics. It was both shocking and electrifying.

Bella let go of her guitar and gripped the microphone in both hands, her knuckles white, while her voice harmonized with Cassie Dean's in one last note before Cassie's solo guitar riff took them to the final lines. The ultimate finale.

Somewhere beneath, all was dark. All was silent.

Momentarily.

ABOUT THE AUTHOR

Gary Lee Vincent was born in Clarksburg, West Virginia and is an accomplished author, musician, actor, producer and entrepreneur. In 2010, his horror novel *Darkened Hills* was selected as 2010 Book of the Year winner by *Foreword Reviews Magazine* and became the pilot novel for *DARKENED - THE WEST VIRGINIA VAMPIRE SERIES*, that encompasses the novels *Darkened Hills, Darkened Hollows, Darkened Waters, Darkened Souls* and *Darkened Minds.* He has also authored the bizarro thriller *Passageway,* a tribute to H.P. Lovecraft.

Gary co-authored the novel *Belly Timber* with John Russo, Solon Tsangaras, Dustin Kay and Ken Wallace, and co-authored the novel *Attack of the Melonheads* with Bob Gray and Solon Tsangaras. Both books are in production to be major motion pictures.

His short story *Glory Holes* appears in *The Big Book of Bizarro.* His short story *The Tailsman* appears in *Westward Hoes* and was recently made into a comic book by Burning Bulb Publishing's comics division. His short story *Cocaine Connie* appears in the *Night of the Living Dead* tribute anthology *Rise of the Dead.*

As an actor, Gary starred as George Pogue in the film *Belly Timber* and played Oscar in the film *My Uncle John is a Zombie.* He has appeared in other films such as *Endor, The Goddess* and *Ayla.*

As a musician, Gary has produced three CDs: *100 Percent, Passion, Pleasure & Pain,* and *Somewhere Down the Road.* A forth musical project, *Passion, Pleasure & Pain 2: The Edge of Forever,* is in the works for a 2017 release.

ALSO BY
GARY LEE VINCENT

BELLY TIMBER

From the writers of Darkened Hills, Detour to Armageddon and Night of the Living Dead comes a novel unlike any other...

In the 1800's, ordinary people learned the secret of the Kala and undertook extraordinary measures to rid the earth of this evil. This is their story.

For John McCormick, life on the Indiana frontier held nothing but promise. His settlement along the White River would soon become the crossroads of America. Friends and family from back in Ohio and other points east were all making plans to see what all the fuss was about in the newly-formed city of Indianapolis. Yes, things were good. John had his general store and his friend George Pogue had his blacksmith business. Claims were being staked and relations with the native Indians were amicable. The town was growing and nothing could be better... or so he thought.

In Ohio, an evil was brewing. The Lecky Family, a group of ruthless Mongolian nomads, had made their way to America and were practicing their cannibalistic religion of Kala with reckless abandon. No one was safe, not even John McCormick's family.

Burning Bulb
PUBLISHING

NOVELIZATION BY
SOLON TSANGARAS & GARY LEE VINCENT

BOB GRAY'S ATTACK OF THE MELONHEADS

"Melonheads is what I love. Give me a body count and gore, but don't forget the laughs. Anytime that I can be reminded of what makes Horror great it is a good thing. Melonheads does that and is something we should all support. Consider it highly recommended."
—*Screamsine.us*

Fifty years ago, a doctor sought to cure a terrible disease. Hidden from the world, Doctor Malcolm Crowe toiled in the dead of night while the world was sleeping, creating a new breed of mutant—all in the name of science.

Yes, he thought he could cure the sick children. But he was wrong.

Today, the results of his cruel and unconventional experiments have manifested into an evil never before seen.

Now, in Kirtland, Ohio, the town's unsuspecting residents are about to encounter the full onslaught of this unimaginable terror.

Can something be done before it's too late?

Burning Bulb
PUBLISHING

GARY LEE VINCENT'S
DARKENED
THE WEST VIRGINIA VAMPIRE SERIES

DARKENED HILLS

When evil descends on a small West Virginia town, who will survive?

Jonathan did not start out his life to become a rambler, it justworked out that way. William was a troubled youth with something to hide. Both were from Melas, a small town tucked away in the West Virginia hills... a town where disappearances are happening more and more frequently.

After the suicide of a wanted serial killer, the townsfolk thought the nightmare was over. But when a centuries-old vampire is discovered they find out the hard way it's just getting started. Dark secrets can only stay hidden for so long and when the devil comes to collect, there will be hell to pay. Can Jonathan and William find a way to stop the vampire before it's too late? Find out in *Darkened Hills!*

DARKENED HOLLOWS

In the heart-stopping sequel to the award-winning *Darkened Hills*, Jonathan and William must return to West Virginia to face possible criminal charges stemming from their last visit to the damned town of Melas, where both had narrowly escaped the clutches of a vampire seethe.

And as livestock start mysteriously getting murdered with all of their blood drained, worried farmers are searching for answers - leaving the local Sheriff and his deputy racing against time to learn the cause before a more violent crime is committed

Burning Bulb
PUBLISHING

WWW.DARKENEDHILLS.COM

GARY LEE VINCENT'S
DARKENED
THE WEST VIRGINIA VAMPIRE SERIES

DARKENED WATERS

When the world goes to hell, the chosen must arise!

As Talman Cane orchestrates a flood of epic proportions in this third installment of the *Darkened* series the towns of Melas and Tarklin are caught completely off guard by the deluge. Hell-bent on finishing what they started, the evil brothers return to the lunatic asylum to take care of the witnesses and add to the ever-growing army of the undead.

Aided by Lucifer himself and the insane vampire demon Legion, the stage is set to channel all of the forces of hell to come forth. In an all-out race to survive, Jonathan, William, and Amanda soon discover they are up against impossible odds as Lucifer opens the Gateway to Hell, ushering in the zombie apocalypse and the End Times.

Find out who will survive this cosmic battle of the ages in *Darkened Waters!*

DARKENED SOULS

Melas and the Madison House are about to be rebuilt.
True evil is about to be reborne!

Young ex-priest and vampire-killer William is drawn back to the West Virginian town that almost killed him, where his vampire arch-enemy Victor Rothenstein still stalks the earth.

The town of Melas lies destroyed after the battle of the End of Days. But why is wealthy Jackie Nixon so eager to rebuild it using the bone dust of murdered souls?

Terrible evil has visited before, but the Gateway to Hell is about to be reopened in a horrific climax. And this time – it's personal.

WWW. DARKENED HILLS.COM

Burning Bulb
PUBLISHING

GARY LEE VINCENT

PASSAGEWAY

When an archaeological dig goes horribly wrong, the team is trapped in an alternate world where evil awaits them at every turn. Find out who will survive the Passageway! Skeleton warriors, zombies, other undead beings and werewolves are all very real inside the Passageway! Embark on a deadly tale that will keep you guessing which path to take as you descend into madness in Gary Lee Vincent's bizarro tribute to H.P. Lovecraft. Passageway will leave you breathless to the end!

www.GaryVincent.com

THE TAILSMAN

From the creators of *The Big Book of Bizarro* and *Westward Hoes* comes a new comic unlike anything you have ever seen!

He's hot on the trail, looking for some *tail...*

Sly Franko was a man of the West, a forger of the wild frontier. Like the Country Western song that would be written years after he died, the words, "Faster horses, younger women, and more money," seemed to be the anthem of this horn dog cowboy.

Franko would ride into town on a blazing saddle, find the closest saloon to wet the whistle, belly up to a good card game, and find him a hot-loving hussy to get his cowpoke on with.

However, Sly might have met his match when a visit to bathroom leads to terror and death. Can Sly and his poker buddies solve the mystery before more of the townsfolk are murdered? Find out in this exciting premier issue of *The Tailsman!*

WWW.BURNINGBULBCOMICS.COM

ANTHOLOGIES
BIZARRO AND TRANSGRESSIVE FICTION

THE BIG BOOK OF BIZARRO

The Big Book of Bizarro brings together the peculiar prose of an international cast of the most grotesquely-gonzo, genre-grinding modern writers who ever put pen to paper (or mouse to pad), including:

NIGHT OF THE LIVING DEAD horror writers John Russo & George Kosana; HUSTLER MAGAZINE erotica contributors Eva Hore, Andrée Lachapelle, & J. Troy Seate and established Bizarro genre authors D. Harlan Wilson, William Pauley III, Wol-vriey, Laird Long, Richard Godwin and so many more!

From Alien abductions to Zombie sex, The Big Book of Bizarro contains OVER FIFTY STORIES of the most outrélandish transgressive fiction that you'll ever lay your capricious and curious hands upon!

WESTWARD HOES

Nine outlaw writers rode into town from obscurity to pen nine tantalizing tales of horror and fantasy, and leaving once they branded their own personal marks on the weird western genre and became living legends of the American Frontier experience.

Like drunken Indian scouts, the writers fervidly tracked down and captured the Western genre, tore off its fashionable veneer and ravished its exposed essence.

So belly up to the bar with your favorite soiled dove and enjoy perusing these thrilling tales of Old West debauchery, danger and desire; compiled by the publisher of The Big Book of Bizarro and featuring the bizarro novella Big Trouble in Little Ass by Wol-vriey.

Burning Bulb
PUBLISHING

RISE OF THE DEAD

AN EARTH-SHATTERING ANTHOLOGY OF ZOMBIE TERROR

Featuring Stories By:

John A. Russo   Tyson Blue   E.L. Stice   Nelson W. Pyles
Andy Rausch   Stephen Spignesi   R.D. Riley   Zakary McGaha
David J. Fairhead   Gary Lee Vincent   David C. Hayes   Rachel Montgomery
Paul Victor Wargelin   David F. Walker   William Vitka
Rich Bottles Jr.   Douglas Brode

RISE OF THE DEAD - a collection of seventeen tales of unspeakable zombie terror. Featuring a foreword and short story by John A. Russo and the short story *Cocaine Connie* by Gary Lee Vincent!

www.TheJohnRusso.com

Burning Bulb
PUBLISHING

WEST VIRGINIA - THEMED
HUMORROROTICA

BY RICH BOTTLES JR.

HELLHOLE WEST VIRGINIA

From the heights of Mothman's perch high atop the Silver Bridge in Point Pleasant to the depths of Hellhole Cavern in Pendleton County, evil lurks within the shadows as the sun sets upon the haunted hills and hollows of West Virginia.

Bizarro author Rich Bottles Jr. blows the coffin lid off horror genre clichés with this tour de force cast of Eco-friendly vampires, beach-yearning zombies and sex-starved she-devils.

LUMBERJACKED

If you are easily offended or do not possess a truly depraved sense of humor, this story may not be the light summer reading fare you desire. As for the four feisty female freshmen stranded on top of West Virginia's third highest mountain, they have no choice but to experience the sick, twisted debauchery and perverted mayhem described deep inside the tight unbroken bindings of this horrific missive.

Lumberjacked takes the reader to a nightmarish world where character development and aesthetic integrity are prematurely cut short by the swinging axes of maniacal lumberjacks, who are hell bent on death and destruction in the remote forests of Appalachia. And at the climax, when paranoia crosses over to the paranormal, Lumberjacked makes Deliverance look like a family raft trip down the Lower Gauley.

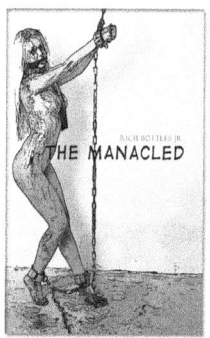

THE MANACLED

What happens when twin brothers lease out the former West Virginia State Penitentiary with the false purpose of filming a documentary on supernatural phenomena, but their true intention is to make a pornographic movie?

Chaos ensues as the disturbed spirits of murdered convicts, along with the reanimated dead from the neighboring Indian Burial Mound, take their vengeance on the unwary and undressed trespassers.

Zombies, ghosts, mobsters and porn collide in this bizarre tale from horror author Rich Bottles Jr.

Burning Bulb
PUBLISHING

JOSH HANCOCK

THE GIRLS OF OCTOBER